CAT IN THE CRYPT

"Bathsheba! Here, kitty, kitty!" Mandy called.

There was no answering meow, no sign of a big tabby cat. Mandy walked around the outside of the church, looking into each dark hollow and crevice where a cat might hide.

James was calling out Bathsheba's name, too, as he ran up and down the rows of tombstones. His voice sounded lost and eerie in the empty graveyard.

Just then, as the moon slid behind a cloud, pitching the church and graveyard into deeper darkness, a streak of light seemed to dart past Mandy. She swallowed hard and turned her head. *What was that?*

Cat in the Crypt

Ben M. Baglio

Illustrations by Ann Baum

Cover illustration by
John Butler

AN
APPLE
PAPERBACK

SCHOLASTIC INC.
New York Toronto London Auckland Sydney
Mexico City New Delhi Hong Kong Buenos Aires

No part of this publication may be reproduced in whole or in part, or stored in a retrieval system, or transmitted in any form or by any means, electronic, mechanical, photocopying, recording, or otherwise, without written permission of the publisher. For information regarding permission, write to Working Partners Limited, 1 Albion Place, London W6 0QT, United Kingdom.

ISBN 0-439-34407-7

All rights reserved. Published by Scholastic Inc., 555 Broadway, New York, NY 10012, by arrangement with Working Partners Limited. ANIMAL ARK is a trademark of Working Partners Limited. SCHOLASTIC, APPLE PAPERBACKS, and associated logos are trademarks and/or registered trademarks of Scholastic Inc.

12 11 10 9 8 7 6 5 4 3 2   1 2 3 4 5 6/0

Printed in the U.S.A.   40

First Scholastic printing, October 2001

Special thanks to Susan Bentley.
Thanks also to C. J. Hall,
B.Vet.Med., M.R.C.V.S., for reviewing
the veterinary information contained in this book.

TM

One

The wrought-iron gate of the crypt swung slowly open. Mandy Hope watched a pale, creamy gray cat emerge from the darkness and walk up the steps into the church. Silently, it walked down the empty nave and slid out of the open front door. In the graveyard behind the church, it paused to look around, its face in deep shadow. Then it laid back its ears and began to call, a strange haunting howl echoing around the graves . . .

Mandy jerked awake and sat up in bed. The dream was still there at the back of her mind, sending little chills prickling down her spine. Over the past two weeks, she'd had the exact same dream almost every

1

night. She shivered and reached out to turn on the bed-side light.

The familiar sights of her own room were comforting, but it was cold now that the central heating was off. She thought of snuggling back under the quilt, but felt wide-awake. Maybe a hot drink would help her to get back to sleep.

In the kitchen she had just boiled a kettle of water and was spooning hot chocolate mix into a mug when a voice behind her said, "Is there enough hot water for two?"

"Oh!" Mandy spun around. "Dad! I tried to be quiet."

Dr. Adam ruffled his daughter's shortish hair. "That's all right, sweetheart. I was reading in bed, catching up on some articles in one of my vet's magazines. What woke you? Was it that dream again?"

Mandy nodded as she reached for another mug. "It's weird, Dad. I mean — how come it's always the same? I'm sure the dream must mean something, but I'm not sure what it is!"

Dr. Adam sat at the kitchen table and propped his chin on his hand. "Hmm. I'm no expert at interpreting dreams, but I'd say something's definitely on your mind."

Just then, Dr. Emily came into the kitchen, looking sleepy-eyed. Her red hair fell loose on her shoulders. "Can anyone join the party?" she joked. "I wouldn't want to miss anything."

Mandy grinned at her mom. "Hot chocolate times three!"

"I heard you talking about these dreams you've been having," Dr. Emily said. "I think they could have something to do with Bathsheba."

Mandy blinked. Bathsheba was the big tabby cat that had belonged to Reverend Madeley. The tabby had been a familiar sight in Walton Parish Church, which was used by Mandy's school for services at Christmas and Easter. Sadly, Reverend Madeley had died a couple of weeks ago and Bathsheba hadn't been seen since.

Dr. Adam nodded thoughtfully. "I think your mom may be right. You were very fond of that cat, weren't you?" he asked.

Pouring hot water into the three mugs, Mandy nodded. "She *was* a great cat. She had this funny, wheezy purr that seemed extra loud when we made a fuss over her." Mandy smiled as she remembered the tabby's eccentric habits. "Bathsheba accompanied Reverend Madeley to every church service, you know. She always sat at the top of the steps leading down to the crypt, where she could keep an eye on everything."

Mandy picked up her mug and clasped her hands around its warmth. "James was very fond of Bathsheba, too," she added. James Hunter was Mandy's best friend. He was a year behind her at Walton Moor School. "It was James who noticed that Bathsheba looked just like the cat gargoyle."

"Cat gargoyle?" her mom asked.

"There's one on the wall, above the crypt steps," Mandy explained. "It's got a round face and big eyes — just like Bathsheba."

Dr. Adam sipped his hot chocolate. "Well, then, I think the case is solved!" he concluded, giving Mandy one of his lopsided smiles. "Take one missing cat, who had the habit of sitting outside a crypt, one animal lover with a vivid imagination — and what have you got?"

Mandy blushed. "Okay. I guess you're right." Her dad's conclusion made good sense. Bathsheba's running away *had* been on her mind a lot.

Dr. Emily put an arm around Mandy and gave her a hug. "Drink up. Then we can all get back to bed."

"And Bathsheba might still turn up," Dr. Adam added reassuringly. "It's not that unusual for cats to go wandering around. Missing pets often turn up right out of the blue, weeks after they first were missing."

"I know," Mandy replied. "I just wish there was something more that James and I could do."

"You two haven't exactly been idle," Dr. Emily observed. "Those flyers you've pinned up on the school bulletin board and in the Walton post office should attract attention."

"Your mom's right, honey," said Dr. Adam. "Try not to worry about Bathsheba for the time being. Okay?"

"Okay," Mandy agreed. It was good advice, as usual. Her mom and dad usually managed to put things into perspective.

A few minutes later, everyone trudged back upstairs.

Mandy climbed into bed and pulled the quilt up to her chin. *Mystery solved*, she thought. Except for one thing. James was as worried about Bathsheba as she was. So how come *he* hadn't been having strange dreams?

Mandy and James were making their way to school the following day. It was a cold January morning. The sidewalks were glistening with frost, and their breath made clouds in the cold air.

"Can you remember what you dreamed about last night?" Mandy thought she'd check James out. If he had seen the pale cat in his dreams, then she'd know that something very strange was going on.

"I certainly can!" James nodded, his face dead serious.

Mandy paid close attention. "What? Tell me!"

"I was at this marshmallow-eating contest," James said in a hushed voice. "It was terrible. I was cramming giant marshmallows into my mouth like crazy. Then I woke up and found —"

" — that you were trying to swallow your pillow!" Mandy finished. "Ha-ha. Very funny."

"Oh, you've heard it!" James grinned at her, his eyes sparkling behind his glasses. "Sorry. I couldn't resist that. Seriously though — did you have that spooky cat dream again?"

"Yes. And this time it woke me up," Mandy replied. Briefly, she ran through what had happened the night before. "But after I went back to bed, I slept like a log. I think talking about it with Mom and Dad helped. They seem convinced that once I stop worrying about Bathsheba, these dreams will stop."

"It's going to be hard *not* to worry about her," James said seriously. "I mean — I keep thinking that she could be lying hurt somewhere."

"Me, too," Mandy replied, shifting her schoolbag to her other shoulder. "Or maybe she's wandered off and gotten lost or locked in somewhere. Maybe she's starving or injured — I don't know which is worse!"

"Well, I think she'll try to find her way back home," James said firmly. "Remember that story in the *Yorkshire Post* last week about a cat that climbed into a van and got driven hundreds of miles away from its home? It found its way back to its owners again! Some scientist said cats can follow invisible magnetic lines or something."

It was a good theory, Mandy thought, *but James was*

forgetting something. "Bathsheba's owner won't be waiting for her, though, James."

"That's true," James said glumly. "Is Mrs. King still keeping an eye out for her?"

Mandy had heard that Mrs. King, the Walton Parish Church secretary, had been looking out for Bathsheba to take her in. "I think so," Mandy replied. "But the reverend's house is all locked up now."

James frowned. "So what would Bathsheba do if she did come back?"

Mandy thought for a while. "I think she'd stay around the graveyard. It would be familiar ground for her. She used to spend lots of time in there, between services."

"That makes sense," James agreed. "There would be mice to catch and somewhere to keep warm."

"But it would still be freezing in this weather." Mandy bit her lip, then she brightened up. "Hey, what if *we* kept a lookout at the graveyard? Then if Bathsheba turns up, we can rescue her."

"Good idea," James nodded, pushing his glasses more firmly onto his nose.

"All right," Mandy said, warming to the idea. "We'll start as soon as school is over. Okay?"

"Okay," James said. "But it'll be getting dark when we leave school. It could be pretty creepy in the graveyard."

"You're not scared, are you?" Mandy joked.

"Who, me?" James squared his shoulders and pushed his floppy, dark fringe of hair off his face. "*No way!* See you later."

Dusk had gathered under the winter sky when Mandy met up with James after school. They went straight to the graveyard.

Walton Parish Church had stood for hundreds of years. It was only a couple of minutes' walk from Walton Moor School.

Mandy and James looked up at the gothic outline of its stone walls and tower, black against the darkening winter sky. The light of a nearby street lamp hardly lit the graveyard at all.

"Just remember what Grandpa says," Mandy said, looking at the assorted tombstones jutting out of the shadows.

"What's that?" James asked.

"The dead can't hurt anyone," she replied, sounding calmer than she felt.

"Oh, right. That really makes me feel better," James murmured.

"Come on," Mandy said, gathering her courage in both hands. "We've been in here hundreds of times in the daylight. Let's go in through the gate."

"Ooh-ee-ooh," James hummed, glancing up as they passed under the roofed main gateway into the graveyard. "This is where the coffin and pallbearers wait for the reverend to arrive," he said in a hollow, spooky voice.

"I know," Mandy said, giving him a shove. "You can't scare me, James Hunter!"

There was a huge elm tree in the graveyard, and the spreading branches cast gloomy shadows over the rows of tombstones.

The grass crunched below their feet as they began looking around. Mandy was thinking that it would be a good idea to bring a flashlight next time, when suddenly a large, pale shape swooped out of the elm tree. It loomed toward them out of the darkness, silent and ghostly.

"Argh!" James gave a strangled cry and almost collided with Mandy. His fingers dug into her arm. "What's that?"

Mandy's stomach clenched with fright. She watched the shape dip low over the graves, then it glided up to the church roof. "Oh," she let out a relieved sigh. "It's only an owl, silly!"

"Phew!" James relaxed his grip. "I nearly had a heart attack just then! Um, do you think we could hurry up? It's freezing, and I'm starving."

"You always are!" Mandy replied. "It'll be quicker if we split up. I'll go and look around the outside of the church. Bathsheba might be keeping warm in a doorway or in one of the nooks and crannies near the bell tower."

"All right. I'll check out these tombstones," James said. "Meet you back here in fifteen minutes? Call out if you find anything."

"Okay," Mandy called over her shoulder as she set off down the frosty path.

The shadows were inky-black under the stone arch-way. As Mandy's eyes adjusted to the gloom, she could see the empty porch and the ancient door — all brass-studded oak.

"Bathsheba! Here, kitty, kitty!" she called as she searched.

There was no answering meow, no sign of a big tabby cat. Mandy walked around the outside of the church, looking into each dark hollow and crevice where a cat might hide.

James was calling out Bathsheba's name, too, as he ran up and down the rows of headstones. His voice sounded lost and eerie in the empty graveyard.

Just then, as the moon slid behind a cloud, throwing the church and graveyard into deeper darkness, a streak of light seemed to dart past Mandy. She swallowed hard and turned her head. *What was that?*

There was nothing there now. Maybe she had imagined it. Mandy was beginning to wish she hadn't suggested that she and James split up.

She was relieved when, a few minutes later, she reached the main gate and saw James waiting there.

"Any luck?" he asked at once. He was blowing on his fingers to warm them.

Mandy shook her head. "I've checked everywhere. How about you?"

James shook his head.

Mandy sighed, disappointed again.

"We could come again on our way to school tomorrow," James suggested.

"Okay," Mandy agreed. "I'll meet you half an hour earlier. That'll give us lots of time to look around."

James nodded. "Great. And I'll borrow one of Dad's flashlights, in case we need to come back tomorrow afternoon."

"Good idea," Mandy said as they began walking toward the bus stop. "I'll bring one, too. My dad's got one in the car, in case the Land Rover breaks down."

The bus to Welford dropped them at the Fox and Goose bus stop and Mandy and James went their separate ways.

Mandy headed for the narrow lane that led to the Animal Ark Veterinary Clinic and pulled her scarf around her cold face. "Wherever you are, Bathsheba," she said under her breath, "I hope it's somewhere warm and dry."

Two

"Over a week of coming here, twice a day," James said glumly as he and Mandy began their after-school search, "and all we've got is frostbite! No one's answered those flyers we put up at school and in the post office, either. I'm starting to think all this might be a waste of time."

"I know what you mean," Mandy said quietly as she stared into the gloom of the graveyard. "Oh!" she cried, catching a sudden movement out of the corner of her eye.

She turned quickly, just in time to see a slim, pale

shape slipping through the trees. "Did you see that?" she asked James.

James looked around. "What?"

Mandy gave a shiver. "I thought I saw something."

"Well, there's nothing there now," James said.

Mandy nodded. James was right. "You know," she said, collecting herself, "I still have this strong feeling that Bathsheba will come back. We can't give up yet."

"I didn't mean that we should stop coming here." James flashed her a grin. "I was just complaining!"

Mandy grinned back. That was one of the things she liked about James; he never stayed grumpy for long. She knew he was just as impatient as she was to find out what had happened to Bathsheba. "Come on," she said. "If we're done here, we might as well go home."

"I guess you're right." Suddenly James stiffened. "Wait a minute. A light just went on in the reverend's house. And did you see that?" He swung his flashlight over to the trees.

"What?" Mandy peered through the trees to where James was pointing. "I can't see anything."

"I can!" James said. "Over there. Come on!" He sprinted away.

Mandy followed quickly. Just then, in the wavering beam of James's flashlight, she spotted something, too.

There were shadowy movements and rustling noises over by the hedge.

She caught up with James. "Careful," she whispered. "If it's Bathsheba, we don't want to scare her."

But it was too late for that. "What's going on?" came a startled voice.

James swerved the beam of his flashlight around in surprise. There, caught in the light, was a young woman holding a toddler.

"Oh, sorry!" Mandy breathed. The little boy's wide eyes stared at them from under a mop of blond hair. "We didn't mean to scare you!"

"I think we scared one another!" the woman said. She looked at Mandy and James, her brows drawing together in a frown.

Mandy suddenly realized how they must have looked, creeping around in the graveyard with flashlights — very suspicious.

"We've been searching in the graveyard for a lost cat," she explained. "Right, James?"

James nodded. "Before and after school."

"Oh, really?" The woman's face cleared. "We came outside to find the cat that was walking around our yard — didn't we, Daniel?" she said, smiling at her little boy. "Perhaps it's the one you're looking for, too."

"Was it a big tabby?" Mandy asked eagerly.

"No. It was a light color. More of a creamy gray," the woman said.

"Oh," James said, disappointed.

"Look, why don't you come inside and have a hot drink?" the woman offered, smiling. "It's freezing out here. You can tell me all about this cat you've lost. I'm Elizabeth Jeavons, by the way. Call me Lizzy — everyone does."

She began to make her way back up the path toward the house. "My husband, Colin, is the new reverend," she continued as Mandy and James followed. "You've already met Daniel, here. He's cat crazy!"

Mandy smiled at the little boy. "Hello, Daniel."

"Pussy cat!" Daniel said promptly, his chubby cheeks dimpling in a smile.

"I'm Mandy Hope," Mandy said as Lizzy led the way into the kitchen. "My mom and dad are vets in Welford, a couple of miles down the road."

James introduced himself. "I live in Welford, too," he explained. "Mandy and I go to school here in Walton."

"Pleased to meet you both." Lizzy smiled. "Sounds like we're almost neighbors!" She pointed to some boxes in the kitchen. "You'll have to excuse the state of this place. We haven't finished unpacking yet and we've got contractors doing work. Kevin and Jim are doing a

great job, but everything's going to be a mess for weeks
to come!"

Mandy saw that Reverend Madeley's dark heavy furniture had disappeared. Piles of light wood, cupboard
doors, and furniture were stacked against a wall. Paint
cans, brushes, and piles of newspaper covered the
kitchen surfaces. Boxes were scattered anywhere. It
was a mess all right, but a homey, welcome sort of
mess.

Lizzy put Daniel in his high chair and gave him a
cookie, then put water on to boil. "Sit down if you can
clear a space," she said cheerfully.

Mandy and James sat on wooden boxes, while Lizzy
made some hot chocolate. Daniel sucked the end of his
cookie, then held out the soggy mess to James.

"Um, no thanks," James said, his face getting red.

Mandy tried to keep a straight face. James could cope
with anything to do with animals. He'd seen animals being born and watched her dad stitch up wounds, but
lively toddlers threw him into a panic.

Lizzy poured the hot chocolate into two mugs and set
them on a tray with a plate of cookies. "I'll just take
these into the living room. I bet Kevin and Jim are ready
for a snack."

She reappeared a few minutes later and took some
cake out of one of the boxes. "Help yourselves." She

smiled. "It's not as good as homemade, but I don't have time to think about baking at the moment!"

After pouring more hot chocolate, Lizzy sat down on another box. "So, who does the cat you're looking for belong to?" she asked.

Mandy helped herself to a slice of cake. "Reverend Madeley," she explained. "Bathsheba's the big tabby that used to live here at the house. Everyone in Walton knew her. She used to go to all the church services."

"Oh, yes," Lizzy said, thoughtfully. "Someone mentioned that Reverend Madeley used to have a cat. It sounds like she was quite a character."

"Oh, she was," James said, munching his cake. "She used to sit at the top of the steps leading down to the crypt during each service. Reverend Madeley used to say she was keeping an eye on everyone." James smiled. "But no one's seen her since the reverend died. She just upped and left."

"Yes, but now, if she does come back, she'll find someone to feed and care for her," Mandy said delightedly. "So she might decide to stay."

Looking uncomfortable, Lizzy poured some milk into a cup and gave it to Daniel. "I'll certainly keep my eye open for a big tabby cat," she said. "But I'm afraid I can't promise anything else."

Mandy stared at her. Did that mean that Bathsheba

was no longer welcome there? She threw a questioning glance at James.

He shrugged his shoulders in a "search-me" gesture.

"You don't happen to know who owns that creamy gray cat that Daniel and I saw earlier, do you?" Lizzy asked, clearly changing the subject. "We heard it meowing, but the minute it saw us, it hightailed into the graveyard. We were out looking for it when you almost bumped into us."

"Pussy cat!" Daniel said, beaming from under a milky moustache. "Pussy cat!"

Lizzy chuckled. "Listen to him! Like I said, he's cat crazy."

Mandy saw an opportunity. "Daniel would *love* Bathsheba, then!" she said quickly. "She has this funny-sounding meow. It's sort of creaky and wheezy. And she's really friendly to everybody."

Lizzy looked even more uncomfortable. "I know what you're getting at, Mandy. I'd love to help, but I think I'd better explain before you go any further. Cats are a sore subject around here. We've talked about getting one. I like them, as Daniel does, but Colin's really not big on the idea. He's allergic to a lot of them."

Mandy and James exchanged worried glances. So if Bathsheba ever *did* come back, she was going to find herself without a home!

"I'm sorry," Lizzy said, sounding genuinely apologetic. "But that's how things stand. I'm afraid Colin was relieved to hear that Reverend Madeley's cat had disappeared."

I bet he was, Mandy thought, raising her eyebrows at James. *That meant he didn't have to think about getting rid of her!*

As Lizzy went to get another cookie for Daniel, a man with a thin face and messy brown hair came into the kitchen, carrying a tray with two empty mugs. He was wearing glasses and paint-splattered overalls.

"Thanks very much for the hot chocolate, Mrs. Jeavons," he said with a friendly smile for Mandy and James. "Hi, there."

"Hi," they replied.

"Oh, Kevin. You haven't met Mandy and James. They've just been telling me about a lost cat they've been searching for. A large female tabby, named Bathsheba. I thought maybe you and Jim wouldn't mind keeping an eye out for her."

"We think she might come back to the graveyard," Mandy explained.

"She used to live at the reverend's house," James added.

"Sure, we'll keep a lookout. No problem," Kevin said. "Jim and I are in and out all day with materials and whatnot. If we see a tabby, you'll be the first to know. Leave a telephone number with Mrs. Jeavons, if you like."

"We will. Thanks very much," Mandy said.

"No problem," Kevin said again. It seemed to be his favorite phrase. "I know what it's like to lose a pet. I'm a real animal lover. I have quite a few of my own."

"Have you?" Mandy said, immediately interested. "What do you have?"

"Have you got an hour to spare?" Kevin said. "No seriously — I've got three cats, two dogs, a garter snake, a rabbit, ten terrapins, a chameleon, and a cockatiel at the moment!"

"Yikes!" James said. "I have enough trouble looking after my cat and dog."

"Are you running an animal sanctuary?" Mandy asked.

"No! Sometimes it feels like it, though!" Kevin chuckled. "My wife, Amy, says we'll have to move to a larger house if I get any more pets. The trouble is that people know I love animals. They bring me any they don't want. And you can't refuse, can you? Amy says I'm a real softy, but I don't care." Looking at his paint-splattered watch, he headed for the door. "Anyway, I must get back to work. Nice to meet you two."

"You, too," Mandy and James replied.

The contractor went back out into the hall. They could hear him whistling.

"Kevin seems to live for those animals of his," Lizzy said. "Especially his dogs. He says they go everywhere with him. He even brings them to work with him."

Mandy raised her eyebrows. She imagined two dogs curled up in the living room, watching patiently while Kevin climbed up and down a ladder with paint and brushes. "Don't you mind?" she asked.

"What do you mean? Oh, I see!" Lizzy chuckled. "He doesn't bring them in the house. They stay outside in his van," she explained.

Mandy had seen a large white van parked just outside the house, but she hadn't taken much notice of it. *That's awful!* she thought, beginning to change her opinion of Kevin. "All day? They must get really bored."

Lizzy shook her head. "Don't worry." She smiled. "Kevin takes good care of those dogs. They're real characters — just like him."

Mandy glanced at James. It wasn't right, keeping two dogs in a van all day and in this freezing cold weather. She decided they had to check this out. From the look on James's face, she saw that he was thinking the same thing.

"Would you like more hot chocolate?" Lizzy asked.

"No thank you," they answered politely.

Mandy was ready to jump up and dash straight out-side, but she pushed herself slowly to her feet. "We should go now or we'll be late for dinner, won't we, James?"

James nodded quickly.

"If you hang on a minute, Colin will be back," Lizzy said. "He'd love to meet you both. And I'm sure he wouldn't mind taking you home in the car."

"Thanks," James said. "But we don't mind catching the bus. We're used to it."

Lizzy saw them to the door. "I expect you'll meet Colin soon anyway. He's speaking at an assembly at Walton Moor School tomorrow morning."

"I can't wait," Mandy whispered, so that only James could hear.

"Um, we really should get going," James said hastily. "Thanks for the hot chocolate and cake."

"Yes, thanks. The cake was delicious," Mandy said, remembering her manners.

At the doorway, Lizzy waved good-bye with Daniel in her arms. The little boy waved his pudgy hand as they opened the front door. "Bye! Bye!" he shouted.

Mandy and James waved back. "Bye, Daniel!"

"Come and see us again," Lizzy called. "We love to have visitors."

Mandy and James waited until Lizzy had gone back

into the house, then hurried toward the contractors'
van.

Mandy shaded her eyes as she peered into the back
window. It was dark inside, but she could see the shapes
of a ladder and other equipment. "I can't see any dogs,"
she said.

James was around at the side of the van. "Me, neither.
This window's all fogged up."

"Hey! What's going on!" a loud voice called out.

Mandy and James nearly jumped out of their skins.
They saw Kevin running toward them, a plastic bag
swinging from his hand.

"Oh, it's you two," he said. "Sorry. I thought it was
kids fooling around with the van. You can't be too careful. There's valuable equipment in here." He unlocked
the back doors, saying, "I bet you want to meet Becky
and Ben. Did Mrs. Jeavons tell you about them?"

Mandy nodded, still feeling anxious. How on earth
could two dogs fit inside this loaded van? She braced
herself for whatever was to come.

"Here you go!" Kevin said, as the doors swung open.
"Meet my two Yorkies. Becky and Ben — short for Re-
becca and Benjamin."

Mandy's eyes opened wide. Nestled in a corner of the
van was a dog basket, lined with fleece. Two small,
sleepy heads poked out from under a layer of blankets.

"Oh, they're gorgeous," she breathed, looking at the tiny faces. Enormous dark eyes peeped out of tousled chestnut fur.

Mandy had been imagining a couple of collies or spaniels, not tiny Yorkshire terriers.

"Time for another walk, guys," Kevin said.

At the word "walk" the dogs jumped out from under the blankets, shook themselves, and trotted happily over to their master, wagging their tails. Kevin took two little plaid coats next to the basket and slipped them onto the dogs, then clipped on their leashes.

Mandy was wondering what Kevin had in his plastic bag. But she didn't have to wait long to find out.

Kevin took out an old-fashioned pottery hot-water bottle. He tucked it beneath the dogs' blankets. "It holds the heat better than those modern rubber things," he explained. "Becky and Ben like to come back to a nice warm bed, don't you two? And in this weather I keep a water bottle tucked in next to them all the time."

The Yorkies yapped and jumped up at Kevin, whom they obviously adored.

"Can we pet them?" Mandy asked.

"Sure, no problem," Kevin said. "Their fur is really soft. They've been coming to work with me ever since they were pups. Now that they're getting older, you'd think they'd rather stay at home in front of the fire,

wouldn't you? But I tried that and they just cried all day. So Amy said, 'You'd better take them with you.'"

Kevin grinned. "I don't mind, really. I go outside, now and then, to make sure they're warm and take them for a couple of walks. And they're as happy as anything."

As she and James petted the dogs, Mandy had to admit that Becky and Ben looked content and well cared for.

"All right, you guys," Kevin said to the Yorkies. "See you later."

"Bye!" Mandy and James gave each of the dogs a final pat. They watched him walk the tiny dogs down the street.

"That's a relief," James breathed. "For a minute back there, I thought you were about to give him a lecture on cruelty to dogs!"

"I would have," Mandy said. "But he didn't need it!"

"You know, Kevin reminds me of someone," James said as they headed toward the bus stop. He had a gleam in his eye. "I can't think who. Someone else who's completely animal crazy."

"Does the person's name begin with 'M' by any chance?" Mandy said.

"Now that you mention it . . ." James was grinning from ear to ear.

Mandy gave him a playful shove.

"Just kidding," James said, rubbing his arm. "Kevin's

great, isn't he? And Lizzy and Daniel are really nice, too."

"Yes," Mandy agreed. "But I'm not looking forward to meeting the new reverend. It's a shame he's not more like Kevin. Then Bathsheba would still have a home to go to."

Three

"So what's the verdict?" Dr. Adam asked that evening as he mixed milk and butter into a pan of mashed potatoes. "Is Walton's new reverend modern or traditional?"

Mandy had just finished telling him about meeting Lizzy and Daniel in the graveyard. She was setting out plates and silverware. It was her mom's turn to do the late clinic, so her dad was making dinner.

"I don't know." She shrugged. "James and I left before Reverend Jeavons came home."

Dr. Adam gave her a questioning look. "Why do I get the feeling that you don't like him very much?"

"Who, *me*?" Mandy said.

"Yes, *you*," Dr. Adam replied. "I know that expression. Come on. Out with it."

"Well — he's probably all right," Mandy said, putting salt and pepper on the table, "if you don't mind cat haters."

"Aha," Dr. Adam said, his dark eyes twinkling. "So that's it. The poor man's already on your blacklist, and you haven't even met him. That doesn't sound very fair to me."

Mandy blushed. Her dad had a way of choosing just the right words to make her examine her conscience. It was really annoying at times. "Reverend Jeavons is glad Bathsheba's missing," she said indignantly. "I don't call that fair, either!"

Dr. Adam opened the oven door and lifted out a cheese and mushroom pie. "Smells good enough to eat," he announced. "I expect there's a reason for the new pastor's aversion to cats."

"Well — Lizzy did say that Reverend Jeavons is allergic to some of them," Mandy murmured.

"Hmm. Allergies can be pretty awful, you know." Dr. Adam finished mashing the potatoes and began to drain a saucepan of green beans. "Coughing and sneezing isn't all that happens. With a bad allergic reaction, the nose and throat tissues can swell up. It's very uncomfortable and sometimes makes breathing difficult."

"Really? I suppose it would be pretty awful if being around cats made you feel that bad," Mandy admitted. *If it wasn't for Bathsheba,* she thought, *I could almost feel sorry for the new reverend.* "I'm just glad I'm not allergic to any animals."

Dr. Adam began dishing out the food. "Me, too," he said with a grin. "Otherwise I'd be looking for someone to take over Animal Ark!"

Mandy gave her dad a mock fierce look. "Don't even think about it!"

Dr. Emily came in from the clinic. She took off her lab coat and hung it behind the door. "Hi, you two. Any luck with finding Bathsheba, Mandy?"

Mandy shook her head. Over dinner, she told her mom and dad about meeting Kevin, and Becky and Ben, his tiny Yorkies.

"He must be devoted to them, to go to so much trouble," Dr. Emily commented.

After clearing away the dishes from the table, Mandy went into the living room and curled up with a wildlife magazine. She loved this room. There was a roaring fire in the big stone fireplace, and red-patterned carpets on the stone floor made the place really cozy.

"I hate to mention it, but haven't you got any homework to do?" Dr. Adam asked an hour later.

Mandy made a face. "Just a little math."

"Shouldn't you go upstairs and do it then?" her dad prompted.

Mandy groaned, but she jumped up and grabbed her book bag. James was a whiz at math, but she really had to work at it!

The following morning, Mandy filed into the auditorium with her classmates.

She saw James sitting in the front row, over by a window, and waved. He waved back, then made a face and pointed to the front of the auditorium.

Mandy turned her head and saw that the principal, Mr. Wakeham, was walking onto the stage. He looked a little annoyed.

"Good morning," Mr. Wakeham began. "We were going to have a special guest this morning, but I'm afraid he hasn't arrived yet." He paused as there was a slight commotion to one side of the stage.

Mandy saw that a teacher was hurriedly ushering a large, broad-shouldered man onto the stage. He had sandy-colored hair and was wearing jeans and a sweatshirt. His friendly gaze swept over the crowded auditorium as he walked over to greet a surprised-looking Mr. Wakeham.

A few seconds later, the principal made an announcement. "Well, it seems that Reverend Jeavons *will* be addressing the assembly. But first, let's give him a warm welcome."

"He looks nice, doesn't he?" she heard someone behind her say.

Mandy didn't want to admit it, but he did. She was caught off-guard. She had been ready to dislike Reverend Jeavons on sight from what she'd heard about him. She'd expected him to be thin and stooped over and miserable-looking — and probably wearing a stuffy suit. But if anything, he reminded her of her own easygoing father.

As Mr. Wakeham went to sit at the side of the stage, Reverend Jeavons smiled at his audience. "Good morning, everyone," he began. "I'm Colin Jeavons, the new reverend at Walton Parish Church. Sorry I'm a little late, but my son Daniel stepped in some paint and I had to help clean up before it dried." He rolled his eyes, then smiled.

There was a ripple of laughter. Mandy noticed that Mr. Wakeham didn't join in. In fact, the sight of the new reverend wearing jeans seemed to have thrown the principal into a state of shock!

"I'm looking forward to getting to know you all," Reverend Jeavons continued. "And once the house emerges from under a sea of paint and dustcovers, I hope some of you will come and visit me and my family."

Mandy found herself enjoying the assembly more than she usually did. Reverend Jeavons had chosen the theme of the lost sheep. Somehow, his version of the story was really interesting. It even made her laugh! Time seemed to fly by.

When the assembly was over, the principal thanked Reverend Jeavons and then everyone filed out and went back to their classrooms.

"Did you see Mr. Wakeham's face when he realized the guy in the jeans and sweatshirt was Walton's new reverend?" giggled one of Mandy's classmates.

Mandy nodded, smiling herself. "It did seem strange, at first. But I like it."

"Yeah! Me, too," came the reply. "It makes him seem almost human."

Mandy laughed.

"Assembly was much better than usual," said another classmate. "Usually it's just boring old stories we've heard before."

As Mandy got her books together for the first lesson, she had mixed feelings about Reverend Jeavons. He had certainly been a big hit with everyone in her class. She wondered what James had thought of him.

"The new reverend seemed okay," James said as they walked toward the graveyard after school. "I mean, he's not a monster or anything."

"No, I guess not." Mandy was still not quite ready to admit that she had liked Reverend Jeavons.

Pausing at the graveyard's main gate, Mandy took her dad's flashlight out of her book bag. It wasn't quite dark, but there were deep shadows between the graves and in the arches and hollows over by the church itself.

"Hello there, you two!" a voice called out. "I thought you might come by."

Mandy and James saw a large figure, holding a much smaller one by the hand. It was Reverend Jeavons and Daniel.

"It looks like he's been waiting for us," James said, looking a bit worried.

"Maybe he doesn't think we should be hanging around the churchyard," Mandy said.

The reverend and his son reached them, their breath steaming in the cold air. "You must be Mandy and James," Reverend Jeavons said. "Lizzy told me all about meeting you here yesterday. She says you've been coming here for two weeks or so."

Mandy nodded. "That's right. We've been looking for Bathsheba."

"Do you really think that cat will come back here now?" the reverend asked. "Isn't it more likely that she's found herself a new family?"

Mandy shook her head. "Not Bathsheba," she said firmly. "This is where she belongs. Isn't it, James?"

James nodded and pushed his glasses more firmly onto his nose.

The reverend looked down at them, a slight frown bringing his sandy brows together. "You two seem very sure about that."

"We are," Mandy said promptly.

"In that case, could you use some help? I have some free time. Daniel and I were just going for a walk." He smiled. "To be truthful, it's nice to be away from paint fumes and sawdust. It's like a demolition site in our kitchen!"

Mandy and James laughed, then nodded.

"Has anyone thought to check inside the church, too?" the reverend asked. "There have been lots of people coming and going around here lately, as we've been settling in — and I, for one, don't always shut the door behind me."

"I hadn't thought of that," Mandy said. Mrs. King, the church secretary, would have checked inside the church when Bathsheba first was missing. Then, during the weeks until Reverend Jeavons had arrived, the church had been kept locked. "No, not recently," she added. But the reverend was right. With all the people coming and going, Bathsheba could have slipped in without anyone seeing her.

"Okay," Reverend Jeavons said. "We'll check inside, too."

Mandy looked at James. "Okay," she said. "That would be great."

"Yes." James blinked. "Thanks, Reverend Jeavons."

"Oh, call me Colin," the reverend said, with a grin. "All my friends do. All right. Where should we start?"

"Well — usually, one of us checks around the graves and the other looks around the outside of the church," Mandy explained.

Colin nodded. "How about if Daniel and I check the outside of the church?" he suggested. "We could meet you by the front door when you've finished checking the graveyard. Then we'll go inside together."

"Fine by us," Mandy and James replied.

Colin swept Daniel up in his arms, then strode off toward the church; a large, bulky figure in his thick coat. They could hear the two of them laughing. Then Daniel's high-pitched voice rang out in answer to something his father said.

Mandy and James did their usual search. It didn't take long. They knew the graveyard by heart now; every tombstone, every crack in every stone block. They checked under bushes and in the hollows of the elm tree's exposed roots.

At one point, Mandy caught sight of a sleek, pale-gray shape just as it disappeared under a bush. She thought it might be the cat that Lizzy and Daniel had seen yesterday. But there was no sign of Bathsheba.

"Brrr," James shivered. "Let's go and find Colin."

"Okay." Mandy was just as eager to get out of the freezing churchyard.

"Find anything?" Colin said as he unlocked the church door.

Mandy shook her head.

"But you're not about to give up?" Colin guessed, his footsteps echoing on the marble floor as he walked down the nave. "I admire your persistence."

The new reverend might not love cats, Mandy thought, *but he was going to an awful lot of trouble to help them look for Bathsheba.*

Ten minutes later, they had searched everywhere: the gaps between the pews, the choir stalls, the little side chapel.

Colin and Daniel came out from a room to one side of the altar. "No sign of any cat in there," Colin reported. "But I think we ought to check the crypt before we call it a day. The wrought-iron entrance gate is always kept closed — but I imagine that a cat might be able to slip

right through it. The spaces between the wrought-iron pattern are a few inches wide in parts."

Mandy and James looked at each other. They hadn't thought of that, either.

"This is where Bathsheba liked to sit," Mandy said as they reached the top of the steps leading down to the crypt.

"She must be a very special cat, for you to care about her so much," Colin said.

"She is," Mandy replied. "She came to all the services. Coming here just won't be the same without her."

Colin nodded. "I can imagine that. But I'd really appreciate it if you'd both come here on Sunday morning."

Mandy and James looked at him questioningly.

"Reverend Hadcroft has kindly offered to bring his Welford congregation over here to Walton on Sunday morning — to support my first service here," Colin explained. "He's really doing his best to make me welcome. The church should be packed with parishioners from Walton *and* Welford. I'm a little nervous actually," he confided. "Seeing a couple more friendly faces in the congregation will help to settle my butterflies!"

Mandy and James smiled. "We'll be here," they promised.

"You will?" Colin beamed all over his face. "Great! I know Lizzy and Daniel will be pleased to see you again." He switched on the light at the top of the crypt steps. The steps and crypt entrance were suddenly bathed in a gentle light. "I'll go down first, and open the gate," he said. "Could you bring Daniel for me?"

Mandy and James nodded, each taking one of the toddler's hands.

"Daddy won't be long," Mandy said to the toddler, who smiled up at her, then watched his father as he went down the stairs.

"Wow! I never realized it was so fancy," James said as Colin opened the wrought-iron entrance gate to the crypt.

Mandy looked down and saw that the entrance *was* very decorated. Two stone angels stood guard, one on either side of an archway wreathed in delicately carved ivy. "Me, neither," she replied. "You can't see it well without the light on."

They made their way slowly down the steps, at Daniel's pace.

"Wow! It's chilly down here!" Colin's voice from inside the crypt came echoing hollowly up the stairs.

"Um, it sounds a bit creepy down there, too!" James whispered. "Are we sure we want to do this?"

Mandy gave him a serious look. It did sound creepy, but if there was a possibility that Bathsheba could be down there, someone should go and see.

Recognizing the look, James squared his shoulders. "Okay. Let's go."

Despite the brightly lit entrance, it was gloomy in the body of the crypt. Mandy smelled dusty old stone and another smell, like dry leaves. A chill crept down her back.

"Yikes!" James said in a wobbly voice. "It's like a cave down here."

It was true, Mandy thought, looking around. *It was much bigger than she had expected.*

The floor was made of huge stone slabs and the vaulted ceiling soared overhead. There were rows of stone tombs, topped with ancient carvings of long-dead noblemen and women. More caskets were stacked in shadowy niches set into stone walls.

"There must be tons of places a cat could hide down here," Mandy said with dismay.

"Cat!" Daniel repeated, recognizing the word.

"Don't worry, we'll help you look," Colin said cheerfully as he swung the toddler back into his arms. "Oh, you might need those flashlights in some of these dark corners. And watch out for cobwebs!"

"I bet there are some juicy spiders down here. We should have brought them a few flies!" James tried to calm his nerves with one of his terrible jokes.

"Ha-ha!" Mandy swallowed hard. She didn't mind spiders in the yard in daylight. But the thought of them dangling from huge webs that were waiting to brush against her face or get tangled in her hair was another thing entirely.

"Are you all right, Mandy?" Colin asked. "You look a little nervous."

"No, I'm fine," Mandy said sharply. "Well, it is a bit creepy," she admitted, smiling sheepishly.

"But it's . . . um . . . interesting," James added, trying to put on a brave face.

Colin chuckled. "Can these be the same two brave kids who've been searching around a dark and gloomy graveyard for the past two weeks? I would think that took some courage!"

Mandy and James grinned. Put like that, the crypt didn't seem so spooky. Daniel certainly didn't mind it. He was hanging onto his dad's shoulder and looking around with interest.

They spent the next few minutes looking into alcoves and behind stone tombs. They disturbed layers of powdery, old dust and even saw a centipede scurrying away to find cover. But there was no sign of a cat.

"Bathsheba! Here, kitty, kitty!" Mandy called out. But no distinctive wheezy meow answered her.

"I don't think she's down here," Colin said eventually, when they'd looked everywhere. "Sorry, guys."

He sounded genuinely disappointed. Mandy couldn't help it. "But, I thought you hated cats!" she blurted out. The thought had been on her mind since Colin first met them in the churchyard and offered to join in the search.

Colin didn't seem to mind. "I'm afraid it's more that they don't agree with me," he replied. "I only have to be in the same room with one and I start coughing and sneezing like an old steam engine! My doctor says I'm probably not allergic to all cats. But I've yet to meet one whose company I can bear for more than a few minutes!"

"What a shame," Mandy said. "Lizzy told us that she and Daniel love cats."

"That's true." Colin nodded. "They'd love one, Daniel especially. But it's just not possible, I'm afraid." Mandy could see the regret in his eyes.

"Anyway," Colin said, cheering up. "Daniel's happy at the moment just to wave at cats that come into the yard — like the creamy gray one."

"Oh," Mandy said. "Has that cat been back again? I wonder who it belongs to."

"No idea," Colin said. "Lizzy puts food out for it, but it never eats anything. So it's probably not a stray. It must be getting fed elsewhere. But it seems to be really shy. Every time Lizzy takes Daniel outside to go to pet it, it disappears."

James hadn't been listening. He was bending over a particularly impressive tomb. "Hey! Just look at this one!" he said eagerly. "It must be really old."

Mandy went over to look. The carved stone figure on top of the tomb wore a headdress that framed her cheeks and covered her chin. Her hands, which rested on the rich folds of her gown, were pressed together in prayer. "Gosh! She's wearing a wimple," Mandy said. "I remember drawing one of those when we studied medieval costumes last year."

"That's right," Colin said. "Some of these tombs *are* very old. This one over here is the first reverend of Walton. He went on to become quite a bigwig in the church. When he died, he wanted to come back to Walton to be buried."

Mandy and James went over to look at the reverend's tomb. On top of the tomb lay a stone, stern-faced figure, dressed in a hooded robe.

"It doesn't look like he was very much fun!" James whispered, just loud enough for Mandy to hear. "I bet he could chop wood with that face, it's so sharp-looking!"

"Don't!" Mandy almost burst with laughter.

"These tombs and carvings are really interesting, though," James went on, more loudly. "It would be great to draw them. Hey! I've just had a super idea."

"Hmm. Sounds like this could spell trouble!" Colin said with a twinkle in his eye.

James grinned. "My class is doing a photography project in art," he began. "We each have to choose a different theme. And I was wondering . . ."

"If you could take photographs down here?" Colin anticipated. "I don't see why not. You can take some in the church, too, if you like."

"Really? Thanks!" James said. "Just wait until I tell the others!"

A few minutes later, they all walked back upstairs. Mandy paused on the top step and pointed upward. "We call that Bathsheba's gargoyle," she told Colin.

Colin craned his neck to look at the stone carving. "Oh, yes. It's nice looking, isn't it? So it must look like Bathsheba?"

James nodded.

Mandy looked at the carving more closely. It seemed to her that the stone face looked sad. It was almost as if, somehow, the gargoyle were also missing Bathsheba.

Four

The following day, Mandy was walking to the playground to meet James at recess when she overheard one of her classmates talking.

"Yeah, it darted right out in front of me as I was passing Walton Church — then just stood there, looking at me!"

"Excuse me for butting in," Mandy said. "But you weren't talking about a cat, were you?"

Sarah, the girl who had spoken, nodded. "Uh-huh. It gave me the scare of my life!" she said dramatically.

"Was it Bathsheba from Walton Church?" Mandy asked excitedly.

Sarah shook her head. "No, I've never seen it before — it was a strange creamy gray color and it had weird, piercing blue eyes." She shivered.

Mandy's heart sank in disappointment that it hadn't been Bathsheba. "What did you do?" she asked Sarah.

"I bent down to pet it, but it kept backing away and wouldn't let me get anywhere near," Sarah replied. "It was a little scary, the way it kept looking right at me — like it was studying me or something. Then it turned away suddenly and vanished back into the graveyard. It's funny, but I felt like it was dismissing me. Like — I wasn't the one it was looking for. Weird, huh?"

Mandy agreed that it was.

In the playground, she told James about Sarah's experience.

"Sounds like the same cat Lizzy and Daniel keep seeing," James commented. "I wonder where it lives?"

Mandy shrugged. "Somewhere near Walton Church, I'd imagine."

"Did Sarah see where it went?" James asked.

"She said it just darted away into the graveyard," Mandy replied.

The bell rang for the end of recess. "I'll be half an hour late leaving this afternoon," James said. "There's a special computer club meeting. Do you want to search the churchyard by yourself?"

"No, I'll wait for you," Mandy replied. "I'll call Mom and Dad to say I'll be a little late."

She didn't want to miss looking for Bathsheba, but she didn't want to look around the graveyard by herself, either!

Mandy was still thinking about the strange pale cat that had been seen around Walton graveyard when the bell rang for dismissal.

She went to meet James in the computer room.

"Hello, Mandy," said Mrs. Ward, the teacher who ran the computer club. "This is a surprise. I didn't think you were all that interested in computers."

Mandy smiled sheepishly. "I'm here to wait for James, actually."

James looked up from his computer and waved her over, but she smiled and shook her head.

"I'll be fine here," she said, sitting down at the back of the room. "I've got an animal magazine I can read."

By the time computer club had finished, Mandy had read her magazine twice. She yawned and stretched as everyone filed past and out of the classroom.

Mrs. Ward walked over with James. "I just had a thought," she said. "Wasn't it you two who put that flyer up about a missing cat on the bulletin board?" she asked.

"Yes," Mandy confirmed. "Can you help?"

"I don't know," Mrs. Ward replied thoughtfully. "It's just that I had a strange experience when passing the graveyard in my car this morning: A cat ran straight out in front of me." The teacher shook her head. "Good thing I was going slowly and was able to stop!" She paused for a second. "But it was the strangest creature. I've never seen a cat quite like it before. A creamy gray, sort of stone color, with the most amazing bright blue eyes. It just stood there in the middle of the road, look-ing at me, then darted away. It seemed to melt into the graveyard wall."

Mandy and James looked at each other.

"Thanks very much for telling us," Mandy said. "But the cat we're looking for is a big tabby."

"Oh, well. Sorry I couldn't help." Mrs. Ward smiled.

Outside school, Mandy fell in step with James and they began walking toward the churchyard.

"*Another* sighting of this strange cat," James said. He shook his head in disbelief. "I wonder why *we* haven't seen it? I mean — we must have been in that graveyard dozens of times now. We practically live there!"

Suddenly, Mandy remembered the time she herself had seen a pale shape running through the trees. "You know — I think I might have seen it after all," she said, thoughtfully. "But where on earth does it come from? And why does it keep going up to people, then running away?"

James shoved his glasses onto the bridge of his nose. "Search me," he said. "It can't be because it's looking for food — otherwise it would eat the food Lizzy Jeavons puts out for it."

They walked on in silence. The cold snap still had Walton in its grip. There were icicles hanging from the drainpipes of buildings they passed. Overhead, the late afternoon sky was a sullen, leaden gray, and the light was fading fast.

The contractors' van was parked outside the reverend's house. They saw that the back was open and a gray-haired man was lifting out a sack of plaster.

"That must be Jim," Mandy said.

Jim nodded as they passed. "Hello there."

"Hi," Mandy and James replied, glancing into the van for a glimpse of Becky and Ben.

Jim chuckled. "I know what you're after. Well, they're not in there. Kevin's taken them out for their regular constitutional."

"What's a consti . . . ?" Mandy looked sideways at James.

"I think he means a walk," James said.

"That's what I said, didn't I?" Jim went back toward the house, chuckling to himself.

"Was that a joke?" James looked baffled.

Mandy grinned. "I think so!"

The gray-haired man had just disappeared inside when they heard an unearthly yowl. Then came the sound of high-pitched yapping and growling.

"That could be Becky and Ben!" James said.

"It's coming from around the corner," Mandy said. "Come on, let's go and see what's happening."

They ran along the street and turned the corner. The churchyard wall stretched a few yards along the side street, until there were some private houses.

Kevin was kneeling down on the sidewalk in front of the wall, trying to calm the two Yorkies.

Yap! Yap! Grr! Becky and Ben jumped around straining against their leashes. They were both out of breath, their pink tongues showing as they panted.

"Easy now, you guys," Kevin was saying. He looked pale and shaken himself. "It's gone now."

Mandy and James raced up to them.

"What's wrong?" Mandy said at once.

Kevin stood up slowly, looking shaken. Becky and Ben were clutched to his chest. "It was that weird creamy gray cat that's been hanging around the grave-yard," he explained. "Lizzy told me about it. Said it was very shy. So when it came running along the graveyard wall toward me, just now, I thought I'd try and give it a bit of attention."

He swallowed hard. "At first, Becky and Ben sat there

good as gold, as usual. They never bark at cats. They've grown up used to all kinds of animals in our house. But that weird cat rubbed them the wrong way. I don't know if it was the bright blue eyes that spooked them, but they certainly spooked me! They gave me the chills!"

Mandy could see that the little Yorkies were still trembling. "I wonder what upset them so much?"

Kevin shrugged his shoulders. "Search me," he replied.

"What happened to the cat?" James asked.

"I didn't really notice," Kevin said. "I was too busy trying to calm these guys down. It just seemed to disappear."

"Just like with Sarah and Mrs. Ward!" James said.

"Who are Sarah and Mrs. Ward?" Kevin blinked from behind his glasses.

"Sarah's a classmate," Mandy explained. "And Mrs. Ward is a teacher. They both saw the cat this morning."

Kevin rubbed his chin. "It's a mystery, isn't it?"

"Maybe we'll see it this time," James said. "We're just about to go on our search for Bathsheba," he explained to Kevin.

"Good luck," Kevin said. "I'd better get back to work, or Jim'll have my head on a platter. Come on, guys."

He put the dogs down on the ground, then moved away, the dogs trotting obediently at his heels.

"See you," Mandy and James called.

"Kevin must have been upset," Mandy said. "He didn't say 'no problem' once."

"It's weird, isn't it?" James said as they retraced their steps. "Somehow we've ended up looking for *two* cats!"

They went through the roofed gate, and Mandy took a deep breath. The graveyard looked somehow unfamiliar today. They were later than usual and, in just the few minutes since they had been speaking to Kevin, it had grown dark. Overhead, the sky was almost black. The tombstones could only just be seen above a veil of mist hovering over the frozen ground.

Mandy fished her dad's flashlight out of her book bag. "This is like one of those old horror movies," she said, shivering. The gray-white swirls of mist seemed to absorb the light.

James clicked his flashlight on, too, and shined it onto the path that led between the tombstones. "Yeah!" he agreed with a chuckle. "Better watch out for ghosts, werewolves, and vampires!"

Mandy giggled. "Sure!"

Suddenly, a haunting wail rose into the air, coming from the direction of the church. The smile froze on James's face. "What's that?"

Her thoughts still full of werewolves and vampires,

Mandy pointed her flashlight toward the church with shaking hands. She half-expected a ghoulish creature to jump out at her.

"Further over!" James gave a piercing whisper and pointed. "Look!"

Mandy moved her beam of light a little to the left to meet James's, then gasped. A creamy gray, smoky substance was oozing out from between the stone wall of the church and the ground. As they stared, it became a

cloud that seemed to hover just above the grass. Then suddenly, the mist cleared around it, and the stone-colored cat they'd heard so much about was standing there, large as life.

Mandy felt a shock of realization go right through her as she met its bright blue stare. "Oh!" she cried.

"What?" James whispered.

Mandy took a deep, shaky breath. "I know this is going to sound unbelievable, but that's the cat I've been dreaming about!"

"Yikes! Are you sure?" James looked as if he couldn't take in what Mandy had just told him.

Mandy nodded. "Its face is always shadowed in my dreams," she explained. "So I hadn't noticed it has the same bright blue eyes people have been describing — but I just *know* it's the same cat."

As if it could understand what Mandy was saying, the cat opened its mouth and let out a whiny cry.

Mandy nodded. "And that eerie meow it makes — it's the same. I should have recognized it."

As if satisfied, the cat slowly turned and began to walk away gracefully.

Mandy felt glued to the spot.

"Come on, before we lose it!" James cried in a shaky voice.

"No, wait!" Mandy hissed. "We'll frighten it!" But it

was too late. James was dashing across the churchyard after it.

The startled cat became just a pale streak. As James's wavering flashlight fell upon the cat, Mandy could barely see it; it was the exact same color as the stone church itself.

"Ow!" James cried suddenly, slipping on the damp grass. He dropped his flashlight and bent to pick it up.

Mandy glanced down at him, saw he was all right, then looked back at the church wall. The cat had disappeared. She swept her flashlight along the wall, but there was no sign of it.

"Oh, no!" James groaned with dismay. "We only took our eyes off it for a second! Sorry. It was my fault it ran off, wasn't it?"

"It's okay." Mandy stood very still. A really strange feeling was creeping up on her. "The cat just disappeared, didn't it? As if it just melted into the stone." She shivered. "And, James," she said in an unsteady voice, "I've just realized something else."

"What?" James said crossly. He seemed furious with himself.

"When we saw it, caught in our light," Mandy whispered, "it didn't seem to have a shadow."

"But that's impossible," James gulped. His eyes were wide and a little scared-looking. "Are you sure?"

Mandy shrugged, not wanting to believe it herself. It was too creepy! "Maybe it was a trick of the light or something," she said, trying to find a reasonable explanation. But that trembly feeling inside was telling her that there just wasn't one.

"I don't get it," James said. "Is this cat real or isn't it?"

Five

Dr. Adam's dark eyebrows rose as Mandy finished telling him all about the mystery cat when she arrived home. Her mom had already left for her yoga class. "You're sure it's the same cat — the one you've been dreaming about?"

Mandy nodded. "I'm sure." Somehow, now that she was at home, sitting in Animal Ark's cozy kitchen, the experience didn't seem so real. But she remembered that awful jolt of shock when she saw the cat. She shivered. "Something's going on, Dad. But what? I can't figure it out."

Dr. Adam came and sat beside her. He put a comforting arm around her shoulders. "To be honest, I'm not sure, either, sweetheart. But there's always an explanation for everything. The trick is to find it."

Mandy nodded, then gave him a shaky smile. "But I'd be happy just to find Bathsheba!" She felt better for having told her dad about her and James's scary experience. He might be as puzzled as she was, but he hadn't laughed or told her she was imagining things.

Dr. Adam kissed her cheek. "That's my girl. Come on. Let's start getting dinner ready for when your mom gets back from her class. Things always look better on a full stomach."

Mandy chuckled as she stood up to help her father. "James would agree with that!" she replied.

"That's because he's got his priorities right. Just like me," Dr. Adam joked. "Don't worry, Mandy. I'm sure we'll get to the bottom of this strange cat business. Like your grandma always says — it'll all come out in the wash!"

"Are you almost ready, Mandy?" Dr. Emily called up the stairs. "We'd better be leaving soon if we're going to get to Walton on time."

It was Sunday morning and the day of the special service. The congregation of Welford Church was to join that of Walton Church to welcome Reverend Jeavons.

"Just a minute, Mom!" Mandy replied, giving her hair a quick brush. She had stayed in bed far too long, thinking about Bathsheba and the mystery cat. Since the cat had shown itself to her and James two nights ago, Mandy's dreams had been different. Now, the cat would come out of the shadows, look at her with its piercing blue eyes, and call to her. *What* was it trying to tell her? To keep on looking for Bathsheba? Not to give up?

"Reverend Hadcroft said he didn't want anyone to be late!" Mandy's mom called again.

"Yes, Mom, coming!" Mandy raced down the stairs and into the hall to grab her coat and scarf.

The four-wheel drive pulled away slowly from Animal Ark, crunching along the still-frozen ground. Along the road that led up to the Fox and Goose crossroads, a layer of white frost coated the bushes.

It was lucky that she and James were both getting lifts directly to Walton Church this morning, Mandy reflected. Yesterday was Saturday, and they had caught the same bus they sometimes used to get to school. But it didn't run on Sunday.

There had been no sign of Bathsheba, though. And no sign of the mystery cat, either. Perhaps today there would be.

"I hope there's a good turnout for Reverend Jeavons's first service," Dr. Adam said, glancing across at her.

"Me, too," Mandy replied. She felt a little nervous on Colin's behalf. It would be awful if hardly anyone showed up.

"Don't worry," Dr. Emily said. "I expect everyone's eager to get a look at the new reverend. Mrs. Ponsonby stopped into the clinic yesterday for some of Pandora's special shampoo. She told me that she's helping Reverend Hadcroft organize rides for people who want to go to the Walton Church service."

Mandy smiled. Mrs. Ponsonby was a large, bossy woman who was very involved in the Welford Women's Club. She doted on Pandora, her spoiled Pekingese. She had another dog, too, a young hound named Toby.

"Oh, well. With Mrs. Ponsonby on the case, there ought to be busloads arriving for the congregation!" Dr. Adam joked.

"Mrs. Ponsonby was not too pleased to see Walton's new reverend wearing jeans when she was introduced to him last week," Dr. Emily informed them, laughing. "You know how she judges people by appearances. She told me that she thinks it's improper for a reverend to wear anything but a suit."

Mandy made a face. She thought of Mrs. Ponsonby's colorful flowery hats and matching dresses. Even her shoes and glasses matched her outfits. Mandy decided she preferred jeans and a sweater any day.

Soon the car reached the outskirts of Welford. On either side of the road, the fields bordered by stone walls looked bleak and windblown. Up on the high hills, there was a dusting of snow.

Dr. Adam glanced across at Mandy. "Did you have your dream again last night?" he asked.

Mandy nodded.

"It's not upsetting you too much, is it?"

Mandy shook her head thoughtfully. "No, not really."

Dr. Emily reached over and gave Mandy's hand a reassuring squeeze. "Mandy's too sensible to be upset by creepy tales," she said firmly. "She gets her good sense from me."

"Oh, really?" Dr. Adam said with a grin. "And I thought she got it from me!"

Mandy chuckled. "No," she repeated more confidently this time, "I'm not feeling spooked today! But I wish I knew what was going on!"

"That's my girl," Dr. Adam said, winking at her.

A few minutes later, they entered Walton, passing Walton Cottage Hospital and Walton Moor School.

"It looks as if Reverend Hadcroft's efforts to get a good turnout have paid off," Dr. Adam said as he searched for a parking space near Walton Church. "There are an awful lot of cars here."

They found a space on a nearby side street. As Mandy

walked with her parents toward the church, she saw
James waiting by the gate. "Hi!" she cried, waving at
him.

James waved back. "Hi, Dr. Adam. Hi, Dr. Emily," he
called. "I thought I'd wait for you here. Mom and Dad
are inside."

Mandy and James stayed together as they all walked
toward the main door. She noticed that he seemed to be
staring at the building more closely than usual.

"What are you doing?" she asked.

"Checking for interesting angles," he replied. "I'm asking the school for permission to come over tomorrow at
lunchtime and take some photographs. Why don't you
ask if you can come with me?"

Mandy made a face. "I might," she said. She wasn't all
that interested in photography, but it would be a good
opportunity to search around the graveyard in daylight.
"Okay, I'll see if I can get permission," she said.

"Great!" James said enthusiastically. "You can be my
assistant."

"Oh, thanks." Mandy gave him a narrow look. "I can
hardly wait."

They had almost reached the stone archway over the
front door when Mandy glanced across the graveyard
toward the house. She saw Lizzy Jeavons and Daniel

come out of the front door and start walking toward them.

"Here come Lizzy and Daniel," she said to her mom and dad. "If you hang on a minute, you can meet them."

Lizzy saw them all waiting. She turned and said something to Daniel, and the toddler raised his arm and waved a gloved hand.

"Hi, there!" Lizzy said as she reached Mandy, James, and Mandy's parents. She smiled at Mandy and James. "Daniel's been really looking forward to seeing you two again. I told him you might sit with us in church if I asked you nicely."

"Of course we will!" Mandy said promptly. "Won't we, James?"

James nodded enthusiastically.

Mandy beamed down at the little boy. "Hello again, Daniel."

"'Lo." Daniel peeped out from beneath a wool hat. His chubby cheeks dimpled as he gave her a toothy grin.

"What a gorgeous little boy!" Dr. Emily said. "How old is he?"

"Two — going on forty!" Lizzy told her wryly. "He keeps me on my toes. Don't you, Daniel?" she said with a fond smile. "You must be Mandy's parents. It's nice to meet you both." She shook hands with each of them in turn. "Let's go inside. It's too cold to stand out here."

As they went into the church, Mandy heard her mom say to Lizzy, "How are you settling in? Mandy told us you're having some work done at the house. That must be a nuisance when you've got a toddler running around."

Lizzy chuckled. "Oh, we're managing. Jim and Kevin, our contractors, are very good. I mean, I could do without the latest complication. They started work on converting the attic into a playroom a couple of days ago. Next thing we knew there were mice everywhere!"

"Oh, no," Dr. Emily said. "How awful."

"Actually, the problem's not too bad," Lizzy admitted. "We haven't seen many mice in the last day or so. Maybe they've found new homes!"

James had heard the conversation, too. "I'm glad I'm not a mouse," he said. "You're all tucked into a cozy nest, then someone comes and kicks you out!"

Mandy nodded. "It's rotten, isn't it?"

As Mandy and James took their seats next to Lizzy and Daniel, Mrs. Ponsonby came sailing down the aisle. She was wearing a fluffy blue coat and a matching hat and scarf. Pandora, her Pekingese, was tucked securely beneath her arm, but there was no sign of Toby, her puppy.

"She must have left Toby at home," Mandy observed. "Perhaps she didn't trust him to behave himself."

"I know the feeling," James said, grinning.

Mandy giggled. Blackie, James's young black Labrador, wasn't the most obedient of dogs.

Mandy and James sat with Lizzy and Daniel on one side, and Mandy's and James's parents on the other. When the time arrived for the service to start, the church was almost full. Reverend Hadcroft began the service with a welcome speech. Then Reverend Jeavons took over. Wearing a spotless white robe, the new reverend announced the first hymn.

Mandy thought Colin looked very snappy. Surely even Mrs. Ponsonby would approve.

The sound of singing filled the old church. Mandy could pick out her dad's voice. He sang in the Welford Church choir. After prayers were said, Colin stepped to the pulpit to deliver his first sermon.

"Daddy!" Daniel piped up. "My daddy!"

There was a ripple of good-natured laughter.

Colin's sermon was great fun. His enthusiasm was infectious. Mandy noticed that even Mrs. Ponsonby was nodding approvingly during the readings. Everyone stood to sing the final hymn.

Suddenly, there was a piercing scream. Mandy saw Mrs. Ponsonby jump to her feet and hold Pandora up with one hand. The Pekingese licked its lips nervously as it swayed in midair.

"Argh!" she yelled, stamping her feet so that her heels clicked on the stone floor.

"Yikes," James commented. "She's almost tap dancing!"

"It's more like a flamenco!" Dr. Adam said with a gleam in his eye.

"Dad!" Mandy almost fell over laughing.

"Help!" Mrs. Ponsonby's loud voice boomed out. "A mouse! It ran over my foot. And there goes another one! This place is *infested*!"

"Uh-oh," Mandy said. "No wonder Lizzy hasn't seen many of the mice from her attic."

"Yeah," James agreed. "They've moved in here."

There was muffled laughter as Mrs. Ponsonby danced around.

"What a big deal she's making," Mandy said with disgust. "As if a couple of teeny-weeny mice could harm a great big human being."

But Lizzy Jeavons looked worried. "Oh, no," she said. "This is awful. Some people are really afraid of mice."

The service was quickly brought to a close. Reverend Jeavons went to the back of the church, ready to shake hands and exchange a few words with each person as they left.

Mandy, James, and their parents filed out of the pew

and made their way out with Lizzy and Daniel. Mrs. Ponsonby barged past in a cloud of strong perfume.

"Ah, Mrs. Ponsonby, isn't it? So glad —" Colin got no further.

"I really object to the mice, Reverend!" Mrs. Ponsonby launched into a lecture. "Mice are filthy things. They spread diseases, you know. And if there are two of them, there are bound to be hundreds more. I was shocked when I saw them. And my poor Pandora is still in shock."

"I bet she is," James muttered, "with Mrs. Ponsonby dangling her in the air and screaming right next to her ear."

Mandy saw that Lizzy Jeavons was trying not to laugh.

"Oh, yes. Thank you for drawing the matter to my attention —" Colin tried to get a word in edgewise, but Mrs. Ponsonby was still ranting.

"It won't do, you know. Mice chew through anything. They'll be running wild. And they breed like, well, like mice. And as for their droppings . . ." She shuddered and her fluffy hat trembled. "You'll just have to get another church cat right away! That's the only solution. Bathsheba would have taken care of these mice."

For once Mandy found herself agreeing with Mrs.

Ponsonby. If the town busybody managed to persuade Colin to welcome Bathsheba back, she promised herself she'd treat her beloved Pandora to a juicy dog treat!

But Colin was made of sterner stuff, and he refused to bow to pressure. "Thank you, again," he said firmly. "You can rest assured that the necessary steps will be taken."

"Oh, well. All right, Reverend." A flutter passed over Mrs. Ponsonby's plump face. "I'm glad to hear it. Goodbye. Lovely service, by the way."

She swept out of the church, her plump little dog held firmly beneath her arm.

"Phew!" Colin said. "She really knows how to chew a person's ear off!" he sighed. "She's right, though," he admitted worriedly. "I'll have to do something about those mice."

"Get another cat?" Mandy suggested hopefully.

"I'm afraid there's no chance of that," Colin replied calmly. "We'll have to find another solution."

Mandy looked at James. They both knew what another "solution" meant. Traps or poison.

"I'll call the pest control people first thing tomorrow morning," Colin decided. "They'll need to come and put out some poison."

Mandy gulped. It just didn't seem right to use poison.

"Now, Mandy," Dr. Emily said gently, seeing her horrified expression. "Reverend Jeavons must do what he thinks is best."

Colin shook his head. "I'm sorry, Mandy. But Mrs. Ponsonby's right about one thing. If she's seen two mice, there are bound to be dozens more. Traps won't be effective enough. I don't like using poison. But it's probably the only way to deal with this problem."

Six

Mandy was dreading seeing the pest control van parked outside the church when she and James passed by on their way to school the following morning.

"Phew!" she said when she saw only the contractors' van outside the house. "Maybe Colin's changed his mind about the poison."

"I wouldn't bet on it," James said. "It's probably too early for Colin to have contacted the pest control people yet."

Kevin was just returning to the van with Becky and Ben. Mandy and James gave him a friendly wave.

The morning passed quickly. Mandy had two of her

favorite subjects. Biology first, then English after recess. She'd asked permission to help James take his photographs and met him at the gate at lunchtime.

"Will an hour be enough to take all your photos?" she asked him as they walked the short distance to Walton Church.

James looped the camera case's strap over his shoulder. "I don't know. I plan to do the ones in the church and the crypt today. We should be able to come back to do the outside ones tomorrow."

They didn't waste any time, but went straight to the church's front door.

Mandy tried the handle. "It's locked."

"I'll go and see if Colin's over at the house," James said.

"Okay. I'll do a quick check around the graveyard while you're gone," Mandy replied.

James went off through the trees, and Mandy began walking up and down between the rows of tombstones. It was much easier to search in the daylight, and she had a clear view across to the hedge.

A few minutes later, she sighed. Nothing — as usual. It had been weeks now since Bathsheba was last seen. Mandy believed that she was one of life's optimists, but even she was starting to think they'd never see the big tabby again.

She saw that Colin was coming over with James at his side. He was carrying a flash and a tripod.

"Still at it?" He gave her a friendly grin.

"Yes, but I haven't found anything," Mandy said glumly.

"Too bad," Colin said sympathetically. "No one can say you haven't tried. Cheer up. Patience is always rewarded."

"I hope so," Mandy murmured.

Colin unlocked the church door and led them inside. "Where do you want to start taking pictures, James? How about the stone screen?" he suggested helpfully.

James looked at the carved stone screen that separated the nave from the choir. "I could do a close-up of the carving. Thanks, Colin. And thanks for letting me borrow your flash."

"No problem," Colin said. "I thought you might need it. Especially down in the crypt. All right, I need to make a phone call — then I'll come back and see how you're doing."

For the next few minutes, Mandy helped James photograph various carvings inside the church. It was awkward adjusting the tripod at first, but she quickly got the hang of it.

"We make a great team. The brilliant, talented photographer and his lighting assistant!" James gave her a look.

Mandy angled the flash so that James could get the best shot. "Don't push your luck!" she said with a grin.

"How are you doing?" Colin reappeared shortly afterward. "Ready to go down into the crypt?"

James nodded, then checked his watch. "Yikes! We've used up over half our lunch hour already."

"Better get a move on then," Colin said with a grin. He picked up the flash. "I'll go and get this set up for you."

Mandy and James picked up the camera and tripod and followed. At the bottom of the steps, next to the crypt entrance, Mandy almost tripped over a small plastic tray. She looked down as the tray's contents rattled. There was a warning label stuck to the top. A few grains of bright blue powder had spilled over onto the ground nearby.

"Mouse poison," Mandy whispered flatly. "And it looks as if the mice have been at it already."

"Poor things. I bet they think it's a tasty treat," James whispered back. "I think it's an awful way to get rid of them. It's a shame that Colin's so against having a cat."

"I know," Mandy replied. "That would be natural pest control. And it would be much kinder to the mice!"

"Come on," James said. "Try not to think about it."

Mandy knew he was right. But that was easier said than done.

Inside the crypt, James got to work. "I'd really like to

photograph the first reverend of Walton's tomb," he said, checking the camera's display to see how much film he had left. "His face is really interesting."

"Okay," Mandy said. She adjusted the light.

James focused on the stern-faced, robed figure, taking photographs from different angles. "That's good. I've managed to get the whole figure in," he said. "These are going to be great!"

One more shot and the camera made a whirring noise as it automatically wound back the used film. "That's it. I'm out of film," James said.

"Great timing," Mandy said. "We've got about ten minutes to pack up and get back to school."

As Colin locked up the church behind them, they thanked him again for his help and for loaning them the flash.

"It was a pleasure," Colin said. "Just let me know if you need to borrow it again."

"Thanks," James said. "Will it be all right if we come back tomorrow at lunchtime to photograph the outside?"

"That's fine," Colin said. "Tell you what: I'll leave the front door unlocked in case you want to photograph anything else inside the church. I have a couple of parishioners to visit and I might not be back by lunchtime. I wouldn't want you to be locked out."

"That would be great," James said. "Thanks a lot."

Mandy and James hurried back to school. There was barely time to hang up their coats before classes started.

"How did it go today at the church?" Dr. Emily asked Mandy that evening. "Did you and James get some good shots?"

"I think so." Mandy nodded absently. "We won't really know until James has the film developed."

Evening clinic was almost over. There were no patients in the waiting room, so she was helping her mom in the treatment room. They were unpacking dressings and stacking them in a cabinet.

Dr. Emily looked up and smiled. She pushed a strand of her curly red hair behind one ear. "Photography doesn't compare with looking after animals, does it?"

Mandy grinned at her mom. "No way!"

Just then the door opened. "Can you fit in one more patient, Emily?" Jean Knox, the Animal Ark receptionist, asked.

Dr. Emily smiled. "I knew the quiet wouldn't last! Yes, of course."

Kevin the contractor walked through the door, holding Ben and Becky in his arms.

"Kevin! What's wrong?" Mandy said, alarmed.

Dr. Emily laid a hand on Mandy's arm. "I expect that's what he's here to find out, sweetheart."

Kevin managed a smile for Mandy, but he looked really worried as he put one of the little dogs on the examination table. She noticed that his hands were shaking.

"It's Becky. I think it's her kidneys," he blurted out. "She's not a young dog and I know older dogs get kidney failure. And it can be fatal, can't it? — Oh, I don't know what Ben would do without her."

"Now — let's not jump to conclusions," Dr. Emily said in her gentle, practical way. "Why don't you tell me Becky's symptoms?"

Kevin gulped and pushed back his unruly mop of hair. Whimpering, Ben cuddled up close to him. Kevin stroked the little dog absently as he began explaining all in a rush. "Well, I stopped at a chicken farm just outside Welford, after I finished work. They sell the freshest eggs there. Anyway, I let Becky and Ben off their leashes to run around in the yard, and I noticed that Becky seemed to be in some pain. And you were the nearest vet. So I rushed straight here, just to be sure."

Dr. Emily nodded calmly. "Very wise. We can often treat a condition if we catch it early. Let's just have a look at Becky."

The little Yorkie behaved beautifully as Dr. Emily ran expert fingers over her. "Hmm. Her bladder is a little inflamed," she said after a few moments. "I think that's what's causing the problem. I'd like to do a couple of tests. Could you leave her here overnight?"

Kevin blinked. "I suppose so, if I have to. The only thing is, she's never been away from Ben. Not ever. She'll miss him terribly."

"Ben can stay, too, can't he, Mom?" Mandy spoke up without thinking.

"We-ell, we don't encourage it," Dr. Emily began. "You know we're short on space here."

"But they could share a cage, and I'll take special care of them," Mandy said persuasively.

Dr. Emily wavered, then she smiled. "All right. It's only for one night. But don't think we're making a habit of this, Mandy."

Looking relieved, Kevin handed Ben to Mandy, then, having nothing left to carry, stuck his hands into his overalls pockets.

He must be really upset, Mandy thought. *He hasn't said "no problem" even once.* "Don't worry. I'll look after them for you," she assured him. "Best room in the house and breakfast in bed!"

Kevin smiled weakly. "All right then. What time should I come by tomorrow, Dr. Emily?"

"Around lunchtime? I'll have the results by then.

Okay? And don't worry, I don't think it's all that serious," Dr. Emily reassured him.

"Really?" Kevin blew out his cheeks. "Thanks. But I know I won't sleep a wink tonight. Bye, Mandy. Thanks a lot."

"All right," Dr. Emily said. "Let's see about those tests, then you can get our guests settled in . . ."

Mandy checked on Becky and Ben before she went to bed and again first thing in the morning. They were curled up together, snug and secure. Two black button noses and two pairs of bright eyes peered out at her from a tangle of chestnut fur.

"Good dogs. You'll be going home soon," she said, petting them.

"Have you got the results yet, Mom?" she asked, popping into the clinic on her way to school.

Dr. Emily smiled. "Now, how did I know you were going to ask that? Yes, I've got the results. It's as I thought. Just a mild infection. I've given Becky an anti-inflammatory injection and put her on some medicine. She's going to be fine."

"So Kevin didn't have to worry about Becky having kidney failure?"

"No. But a worried owner's a caring owner," Dr.

Emily replied. "Give me a worrier, any day. Unless it's Amelia Ponsonby, of course!"

Mandy giggled. "Bye. See you later!" She felt all bright and bubbly as she went out of the front door. It always gave her a great feeling to know a sick animal was going to get better. That was one of the reasons why she wanted to be a vet when she was older.

Lunchtime came around, and Mandy and James went back to the churchyard.

Mandy found looking for good angles and shots quite interesting at first. But twenty minutes later, she was starting to find aperture speeds and automatic focus rather boring. Her mind wandered, and she began wondering whether Kevin had picked up Becky and Ben yet.

James craned his neck, squinting up at the weather vane on the church roof. "I can't seem to get the focus right for this," he commented. "I think I need a more powerful lens."

"Maybe you should go for something closer?" Mandy suggested.

"Good thinking." James turned the camera to one of the decorative arched windows. "Oh, darn! That's no good, either. That huge elm tree is casting a shadow."

"Would you like me to move it out of the way?" Mandy offered helpfully.

"Ha-ha, very funny. Let's move farther back. I want to take some shots of the archway over the door."

"All right." Mandy sighed. It began to rain again. *Oh, great!* she thought. She found herself thinking of warm classrooms and the vending machine in the school hallway that dispensed hot chocolate.

James gave her a pleading look. "Just a couple more. Then we'll have to stop anyway."

Just then, Mandy heard a faint sound. "What's that?" she said. "Listen."

"What? I didn't hear anything," James replied, fiddling with his focus.

Mandy tensed. "There it is again!" A haunting wail floated toward them on the wind. Mandy felt the hairs on the back of her neck stand up. She glanced at James and saw that he'd heard it this time.

"I think . . . it's coming from . . . inside the empty church," James said. "It sounds like —"

"The stone-colored cat!" Mandy finished.

The hollow sound, echoing through half a yard of solid stone, was getting louder. Mandy's imagination went into overdrive. In her mind's eye, she saw lids of stone caskets opening in the crypt as the ancient residents stirred to the unearthly cat's call.

James quickly backed away from the wall and banged

into Mandy, who was still fantasizing about ghastly happenings in the crypt.

"Argh!" she yelled, almost jumping up in the air.

"Sorry!" James said, then knocked the tripod over.

The wind blew stinging raindrops into Mandy's eyes. She looked away — and caught sight of something moving over by the evergreen bush. She blinked hard. No — she wasn't imagining it. "James," she croaked.

"Hang on a sec, Mandy." James was brushing mud off the tripod. "I'll get detention for this if I'm not careful!"

But Mandy hardly heard him. She was watching a cat crawling slowly out from under the hedge. First a rounded face and two flattened ears had appeared, now all of its skinny body emerged. The cat shook itself, so that its fur stood out in damp spikes. Though it was thin and ragged looking, and its tabby coat was dark with rainwater and mud, Mandy would have known it anywhere. *Bathsheba!*

"James!" It came out as another dry croak. "James, look!" Mandy said more loudly, reaching a shaking hand toward him.

"What?" James finally spun around as Mandy tugged insistently at his coat sleeve. He was just in time to see Bathsheba running off toward the entrance of the church. James's mouth dropped open. "Hey! That looked like . . . It couldn't have been . . . could it?"

"Bathsheba! Yes, it was!" Mandy cried.

As if to prove Mandy's words, they heard a familiar wheezy meow. "Listen to that!"

"Yikes!" James said, almost dropping his camera. "It's Bathsheba all right!"

Then, as if in answer to Bathsheba, the plaintive call of the stone-colored cat rang out again from deep within the church.

"Come on!" Mandy called, hurtling in the same direction as Bathsheba. "After those cats!"

Seven

As Mandy rounded the bell tower, she caught a glimpse of Bathsheba dashing awkwardly into the stone entrance. She sprinted forward again, James almost at her heels. He was hanging on tightly to his camera case, which was bumping around as he ran.

Moments later, Mandy and James reached the big oak door themselves. It was slightly ajar. Mandy remembered that Colin had said he'd leave it unlocked for them.

The plaintive calling of the stone-colored cat suddenly drifted away. And, in its place, a different noise began to ring out: a distinctive wheezy meow.

Mandy and James looked at each other. "Bathsheba!" they said together. They dragged the heavy oak door fully open and went inside.

The anxious meows and wails seemed to fill the church. Mandy grabbed James's arm. "Let's go slowly," she warned. "We have to be careful not to alarm her in the distressed state she's in. Don't make any sudden movements or noises."

James nodded. "I bet I can guess where she'll be," he said. He pointed in the direction of the crypt steps.

They walked slowly over there, softly calling Bathsheba's name. The breathy meowing seemed to grow even more urgent.

The top of the crypt steps came into view and, sure enough, a small, dark shape was crouching at the top of the steps.

"Bathsheba! Hello, girl!" Mandy called softly.

As soon as the tabby saw Mandy and James, she opened her mouth wide and gave another plaintive howl. *Meow-ow-ow!*

Mandy couldn't stop herself from hurrying over. She was anxious to find out if the tabby was all right. "Oh, you good girl," she said softly. "You remembered your favorite place." Her heart went out to the cat. Bathsheba was so thin, and her coat was full of thorns.

"Poor thing," said James. "She looks half-starved."

Bathsheba pushed herself awkwardly up to a standing position. Then, looking straight at Mandy and James, the pupils enormous in her green eyes, she flicked her tail and darted away, down the crypt steps.

"Oh, no!" Mandy cried. "She's running away from us! But she needs help!"

They hurried down the steps after her. The crypt entrance was in shadow. The stone angels guarding the archway seemed to loom over them.

And there, on the cold stone floor, was Bathsheba — crouching beside a small, still form.

Mandy drew in her breath sharply. "Oh, no! James — look! It's little Daniel!" She threw herself down beside the unconscious toddler, her heart pounding. "It looks like he might have fallen down the steps!"

"We'd better not move him, in case he's broken something," James said, white-faced. "You stay here; I'll go and get help." He turned to run back up the steps.

"Wait a minute!" Mandy called. There was an overturned plastic tray lying near Daniel's outstretched arm. She picked it up and shook it. Almost empty. A couple of grains of blue-dyed powder fell on to the floor. She remembered kicking the tray the day before. Then it had been almost full. A horrible suspicion crept over her.

She bent right down to get a closer look at the toddler's face. There were dark blue stains around his mouth. "Daniel's not unconscious because he's fallen down the steps and knocked himself out," she cried. "It's because he's eaten mouse poison!"

James and Mandy kneeled beside Daniel's unconscious body. They looked at each other in dismay.

"If nothing's broken, it should be okay to move him," decided James. "I'll push, you pull."

Mandy nodded. Together, they rolled Daniel over on to his back.

"Yikes! He looks awful!" James's mouth was tight with concern. "Is he . . . is he still breathing?"

"I'm not sure." Although Mandy's hands shook, she felt herself grow calm. She remembered all the times she had watched her mom and dad deal with animal emergencies. She had to help Daniel.

Quickly, she checked to see if Daniel was breathing. "Yes," she replied in relief. "But it's rapid and shallow, which I don't think is good." She scooped Daniel up in her arms. "There's no time to waste!"

James ran ahead up the steps. "We'll take turns carrying him," he said. "Tell me when you want me to take over."

Panting, Mandy nodded. For such a little boy, Daniel was surprisingly heavy. She trudged on, ignoring the burning in her leg muscles. Daniel's blond head sagged against her as she ran up the nave. A sudden thought struck her.

"James!" she said without relaxing her stride. "Can you bring what's left of the poison, please? The hospital will need to know what Daniel's swallowed."

"Good thinking!" James dashed back down to the crypt.

Mandy didn't stop to wait for him. She clutched the toddler to her chest and rushed out of the church and toward the house.

As the wind and rain swirled around her, Daniel stirred and gave a soft moan.

Oh, please, Mandy prayed to herself, her eyes filling with tears. *Please let us have found him in time!*

"Do you want me to take Daniel?" James asked anxiously as he caught up with her. Mandy nodded. Daniel's weight was beginning to make her arms really ache.

"Mandy! James!" a voice called.

Mandy gave a sigh of relief. Lizzy Jeavons was rushing up to them.

"Oh, thank goodness you've found Daniel," Lizzy said. "I've been searching for him everywhere. What's happened, has he fallen down?" She broke off, suddenly realizing that something was very wrong.

"He's eaten mouse poison," Mandy said urgently. "Look — you can see the blue dye around his mouth."

"Mandy thinks he ate almost a whole tray," James put in.

"Poison? Oh, no!" Lizzy gasped in shock, reaching out to take her son. "Give him to me now, Mandy. Has he said anything at all?"

Mandy shook her head. "He was unconscious when we found him. I checked his breathing. But we didn't know what else to do."

"Don't worry. You did just the right thing," Lizzy said. She was taking deep breaths, fighting to keep calm. "There's no time to call an ambulance. We'll take him straight to the hospital. Would you two please run ahead and ask Colin to get the car ready?"

"Right." Mandy and James ran toward the house.

"I thought he wasn't going to be back until after lunchtime," James said.

"He must have finished his parish visits early!" Mandy took a short cut across a flower bed. "Good thing, too!"

The back door of the house was unlocked, and they shot straight in. Colin was sitting at a table in the unfinished kitchen. He looked up from working at his computer.

"Whoa there, you two! Where's the fire?" He dragged

his fingers through his thick, sandy hair and gave them his usual friendly grin.

"Lizzy needs you to get the car ready!" Mandy burst out at once. "Daniel needs to go to hospital! He's eaten mouse poison!"

"Oh, no! How on earth did he get inside the church?"

"The door was open when we arrived," Mandy said.

"But I'm sure I latched it." Colin said, looking puzzled. "Or, at least, I think I did. I can't remember now."

He jumped to his feet, grabbed his car keys from a wall hook, and hurled himself through the open back door.

Mandy and James followed him outside. Colin had the car door open and the engine running just as Lizzy raced down the path holding Daniel.

Seconds later, Lizzy and Daniel were climbing into the backseat. Mandy ran forward and closed the car door behind them.

"Oh, I almost forgot." At the last moment, James thrust the almost empty poison container in through the open car window. "We thought you might need this."

Colin put the tray on the front passenger seat. "Thanks, you two," he said in a shaky voice. "Will you be all right here?"

"Yes. You just go." Mandy searched for the right words. "I hope Daniel will be okay."

Colin managed a bleak smile. "So do I."

There was no more time to talk. The car sped away toward the hospital.

Mandy felt her legs almost give way. She staggered into the kitchen and sat down.

James sat down heavily, too. He was as white as a sheet. "Do you think Daniel will be all right?" he asked.

"I don't know," Mandy said worriedly. "But the hospital will know what to do." Suddenly, she sat up straight. "Bathsheba!" she cried. "What about Bathsheba? She might still be in the church!"

James jumped up. "Let's go and find out!"

The tabby was in her favorite place, at the top of the crypt steps. "Look at her. All curled up asleep," Mandy said with relief.

One of Bathsheba's ears twitched, then her eyes opened. She lifted her head and blinked in confusion. Mandy kneeled on the steps and began petting the cat's broad head. "Hello, there girl," she breathed. "Welcome home."

Bathsheba managed a weak, wheezy purr, but a tremor ran over her thin body.

"Oh, my goodness," Mandy sighed. "Look at her!"

"Poor thing." James frowned, looking puzzled. "She seemed all right a few minutes ago, but she seems really weak now."

Mandy leaped to action. She slipped her hands beneath Bathsheba and gently lifted her. She felt the tabby trying to stand up, but her legs seemed all wobbly. "Come on — let's take her into the house. I'm going to call Animal Ark." For the second time that day, Mandy found herself hurrying for help.

Dr. Emily listened in silence as Mandy finished explaining. "... so we went back to get Bathsheba, after Colin and Lizzy took Daniel to the hospital, and now she's here, with us, in the house. She's really thin and weak."

"Well," her mom said. "Thank goodness Daniel's getting expert treatment. Sounds like you and James have been pretty busy! You two stay there. Your dad's taking afternoon clinic and I'm on call, so I'll come straight over. I'll be about ten minutes."

"Okay, Mom." Mandy put the phone down. "Mom will be here soon," she said to James. Mandy looked down at Bathsheba, curled up on James's lap.

"She's so thin," he said. "You can feel her ribs and all the bumps on her backbone. And her coat's full of thorns. But *phew!*" James wrinkled his nose. "She smells a little, too!"

"She can't help it," Mandy said defensively. Mandy began combing the thorns and bits of twig out of the cat's fur with her fingers. But it was no use. Bathsheba needed a full grooming job. Comb, brush, bath — the works.

"Poor girl," James crooned, rubbing the cat under her chin. "I wonder when she last had a good meal."

Mandy shook her head. She frowned. "You know what I don't get?"

"No, what?" James asked.

"Why, after all these weeks, did Bathsheba come back when she did?" Mandy said. "How did she know help was needed?"

James looked a bit uncomfortable. "Well, there is one possibility," he said. "But it's a creepy one."

"Go on," Mandy said, curiously.

"Perhaps the stone-colored cat called her back," he suggested.

A few minutes later, Dr. Emily pulled up outside in her four-wheel drive. She came quickly into the house, carrying a cardboard pet carrier. "Are you two all right?" she asked at once, putting the carrier on the table. "It must have given you both quite a shock, finding Daniel like that."

Mandy nodded, suddenly close to tears and very glad to see her mom. "It did. He looked so small, lying all crumpled up on the floor like that. His little face was all white and pinched."

Dr. Emily gave her a cuddle. "Try not to think about that. He's in good hands now. It's up to the hospital now, okay?" She turned and smiled at James. "You two did really well. Your quick thinking could make all the difference. Poor Colin and Lizzy. They must be frantic with worry. I only hope Daniel will be all right."

"Me, too," Mandy and James both replied.

"All right," Dr. Emily said. "Let's have a look at this feline casualty. This one, I *can* do something about." She bent down and gently picked up Bathsheba.

Mandy watched as her mom examined the cat, searching for signs of wounds or infections.

"Hmm. She's just skin and bones. It looks like she's been through a lot," Dr. Emily judged. "She probably needs liquids before anything else."

"But will she be okay?" Mandy asked.

"I can't see any obvious signs of infection. But I'll give her a more thorough examination once I get her back to Animal Ark," Dr. Emily replied. She gave Bathsheba a friendly pat. "Up you go, girl," she said, lifting her into the pet carrier.

"Can we come back to Animal Ark with you?" Mandy asked. She wanted to make sure that Bathsheba was given the all clear. Then she planned to get her settled in comfortably. After her ordeal, the cat deserved the warmest spot in the residential unit and a dish of food.

"Aren't you and James supposed to be somewhere else?" her mom asked, with a wry grin. "Like school? I don't suppose either of you thought to call and explain your absence?"

Mandy shook her head. "There wasn't time. It was an emergency."

"Hmm," Dr. Emily murmured. "Even so —"

"Uh-oh!" James clapped his hands to his mouth. "I've just realized. I bet we're in big trouble because we didn't show up for afternoon attendance!"

Mandy groaned. "Oh, no. I didn't think about that, either. They probably have search parties out for us and everything!"

"Dog teams, snow sleds, choppers." James took things one step further.

Dr. Emily chuckled. "Hardly! But I expect the school must be getting concerned. I'll give them a call and explain why you'll be returning late."

"Do we have to go back?" Mandy pleaded, her blue eyes wide. "It's only for a couple of hours."

"Yes, you do," Dr. Emily said firmly. "I'm going back to Animal Ark — alone. And we'll have to lock up the house behind us. So you can't stay here."

Mandy sighed. Sometimes she might be able to get around her soft-hearted dad, but her mom was different. Dr. Emily was gentle and caring, but she knew when to be firm.

Dr. Emily went off to make the phone call. She returned a couple of minutes later. "All taken care of," she said. "I spoke to your principal. He was very interested to hear about your rescue mission. He seems to think you're both heroes."

Mandy groaned softly. She looked at James, imagining some kind of awful show-and-tell session in front of the whole school. How embarrassing!

"Do you want to bring Bathsheba out to the car, Mandy?" Dr. Emily asked. "I'd better get back to the clinic and check her right away. I'm likely to get called out at any time. And it's Simon's day off." Simon was the veterinary assistant.

As Mandy picked up the pet carrier, Bathsheba gave a low wail. Mandy slipped her hand inside the carrier and petted her reassuringly. "I'll come and see you the second I get back from school," she promised.

They all walked out to the driveway. Dr. Emily hung back a moment to make sure the house was locked, then she stowed the carrier in the back of the car.

"Bye, sweetheart," she said, to Mandy, kissing her cheek. "See you after school. Bye, James."

"Bye, Dr. Emily. And thanks," James said politely.

"Meet you here later?" James said to Mandy, at the school gate. "I'll come back to Animal Ark with you and check up on Bathsheba. At least we won't have to go searching in that creepy graveyard anymore!"

"Oh, yes!" Mandy nodded, brightening. "There's no need, now."

Luckily, the conversation with the principal was brief

and less embarrassing than Mandy had imagined. She
and James went off to their separate classes.

Mandy took out her math book and spread it open on
her desk. But she knew there was no way she was going
to be able to concentrate. All she could think about was
Bathsheba: returned — but now homeless.

Eight

"Hi, Jean. Where's Mom?" Mandy asked Animal Ark's receptionist, the moment she and James got through the clinic door.

"Hello, you two!" Jean Knox said cheerfully. "Your mom just got back from one of those isolated farms a few miles away. I think she's in the treatment room."

"Thanks," Mandy said. "We'll go straight through."

"Busy afternoon, Mom?" Mandy asked. "Jean said you'd been called out."

Dr. Emily was wearing her white lab coat. She nodded. "A ewe miscarried twin lambs. They didn't survive,

I'm afraid. But I've checked the mother over, and she'll be fine."

"Oh." Mandy hated to hear of any animal dying. But she knew it was fairly common for sheep to miscarry. Their next lambs were almost always all right.

"On a brighter note, your friend Kevin's been in to pick up his Yorkies," her mom continued. "He was so happy when I told him Becky was going to be fine."

"That's great," Mandy said. "Now all we have to do is get Bathsheba well. Can James and I see her?"

Dr. Emily nodded. "I've put her out back in the quarantine room. Just for a couple of days."

"Has she got something contagious, Dr. Emily?" James asked.

"I don't think so," Dr. Emily replied. "But she could be incubating something. It's best not to take chances. Stray cats can pick up all kinds of things."

Bathsheba was curled up on a blanket in her heated cage. As soon as she saw Mandy and James, she gave one of her special loud meows.

"She recognizes us!" James said.

"Of course she does!" Mandy said, opening the door and giving Bathsheba a hug.

Dr. Emily smiled. "She's a lot more comfortable now. But she's badly undernourished. She's going to need to eat little and often until she puts on some weight."

"Did you have to give her any treatment?" Mandy asked.

"I've given her a vitamin injection and a pill in case she has worms," Dr. Emily replied. "And she's eaten a dish of kitten food. But that's all. It's amazing really that she doesn't seem to have caught even a sniffle."

"That's wonderful!" Mandy said happily. She'd been imagining all kinds of complications. "So, all she needs is lots of food!"

"And TLC!" James said. "My dad says that's the best medicine."

"He's right!" Dr. Emily went over to a sink and washed her hands with antibacterial soap. "You two can stop worrying now. Bathsheba's going to be fine."

"Except that she's homeless," Mandy said quietly. She gave Bathsheba a final hug, before closing the cage door.

"Hello, you two. I thought you'd be in here." Dr. Adam came in. He was followed by Reverend Jeavons. "I met Colin here on the driveway. He's got something to tell you."

Colin was beaming. "Daniel's going to be fine. He's a bit groggy and he has a stomachache, so they're keeping him in overnight, but only for observation. Lizzy's staying with him, so I've come home to get a few things for her. I thought I'd just stop by and give you two the good news."

"That's just great. Isn't it, James?" Mandy said.

"Yeah. It's terrific," James said, smiling.

"It certainly is," Dr. Emily agreed. "Daniel's a very lucky little boy."

"It was a close call, though," Colin said seriously. "I feel just terrible about leaving the church door unlatched. Daniel was obviously able to push it open. I'd never have forgiven myself if the worst had happened." He broke off to run his hands through his hair. "Anyway — luckily for all of us, the doctor thinks Mandy and James found Daniel just in time. Another half an hour and it might have been too late."

Mandy suddenly felt cold all over. She hardly dared think about what might have happened.

"And your quick thinking, suggesting we take along the remains of the poison, really helped," Colin informed them. "The doctor was able to identify the type of poison and give Daniel the necessary treatment immediately."

"That was Mandy's idea," James said generously.

"Well, it was a real brainstorm." Colin smiled down at her. "Thanks a lot, Mandy. And you, too, James. Lizzy and I are very, very grateful to you both. You'll never know just how much."

James blushed to the roots of his hair. "That's okay," he said.

Mandy shifted her feet. She always got embarrassed when people thanked her. "Anyone would have done the same," she murmured.

"I'm not sure they would have," Colin said. "In that situation, most people would have panicked. And that includes a few adults I can think of!"

"Our Mandy's got a level head on her shoulders," Dr. Adam said proudly, ruffling his daughter's hair.

Colin folded his arms and leaned back against the shelf. Behind him, in her cage, Bathsheba curled up and went to sleep. "One thing still puzzles me, though. How did you two manage to find Daniel? You'd finished taking photographs in the crypt, hadn't you, James?"

James nodded.

"We weren't planning to go anywhere near the crypt," Mandy explained. "We only went down there after Bathsheba. We saw her running into the church after that strange stone-colored cat."

"We guessed she'd have gone to her favorite place — and there she was," James continued. "But she wouldn't come when we called her — she ran down the steps leading to the crypt, so we followed her and found Daniel."

"So you see," Mandy said slowly, "it wasn't me and James who saved Daniel's life. It was Bathsheba. She *led* us to him!"

Colin shook his head slowly. "It's an incredible story. I don't know what Lizzy's going to make of it when she hears about this."

"She'll probably be as puzzled as the rest of us," Dr. Adam said, scratching his head. "I haven't got a clue about what to make of this."

"But it's all true, Dad," Mandy said. "Isn't it, James?"

James nodded. "*Strange*, but true," he corrected in a hollow voice.

Colin scratched his head again, at a loss. "Well, I'd better be going," he said. "I promised Lizzy I wouldn't be long. I said I'd take her some sandwiches and a Thermos of soup. Hospitals aren't exactly known for their good food!"

"I'd better go home now, too," James said. "Dinner will be ready."

"I'll take you home if you like," Colin offered. "It's on the way."

Mandy walked with James and Colin to the front door.

"Do you think it would be okay if Daniel comes to see Bathsheba?" Colin said to her, pausing in the doorway. "I'm sure Lizzy would like to visit her, too, especially after what she's done for us."

"'Course it's okay!" Mandy said. "Mom and Dad won't mind. They can come anytime."

"Thanks," Colin said. "Thanks again, for everything. Bye, now. See you soon."

Mandy was thoughtful as she went into the kitchen. Her dad was clearing the newspapers from the kitchen table, while her mom was getting dinner ready.

"Uh-oh!" Dr. Adam said with a twinkle in his eye. "I know that look!"

"What do you mean?" Mandy said innocently.

"You're plotting something, Mandy Hope. Out with it!"

Mandy grinned. "It's nothing really. I was just wondering what was going to happen to Bathsheba now. I mean — she can't go back to the reverend's house. We'll have to try and find a home for her, won't we?"

"I thought that might be it." Dr. Adam sighed. "I expect you're racking your brains trying to think of someone to adopt her? You've done all you can for her, sweetheart. We'll call one of the cat rescue organizations and let them take care of it, okay?"

"I suppose so." Mandy sank into a chair and cupped her chin in her hands. Poor Bathsheba. She deserved a good home after all she had been through. But she was going to have to stay in a cage in an animal shelter until someone adopted her.

"Tell you what." Dr. Emily looked up from chopping carrots. "How about if we allow Bathsheba to stay with us in the house until she's fully recovered? But only until then, okay? That will give us time to find a home for her."

"You mean it?" Mandy jumped up. She went over and gave her mom a huge hug. "Thanks a million, Mom. Wait until I tell James!"

It wasn't an ideal solution. But she was going to make the most out of having Bathsheba around — if only for a short while.

A couple of days later, Bathsheba was ready to leave her cage. Mandy and James were getting her settled into a box in the kitchen for the rest of her stay.

Mandy folded a piece of old blanket and put it into a small cardboard box. "There. That makes a cozy bed. What do you think, Bathsheba?"

The tabby was crouched on the red-patterned rug. She looked up at the sound of her name, then trotted over to investigate the box.

James watched her sniffing the cardboard and pawing at the blanket. "She's scent-marking. I think she likes it."

Mandy, meanwhile, spread newspaper on the stone floor, then forked cat food into a bowl. As soon as Bathsheba smelled the food, she forgot about her bed. She walked straight over and began eating.

"Gosh! She's finished it already!" James said a couple of minutes later.

Bathsheba licked her lips, then sat down on the rug and began washing herself meticulously. She was lying stretched out on the rug when the door opened and Dr. Adam poked his head into the room.

"Visitors for you," he announced.

"Hi, you two." Lizzy came into the room, holding Daniel by the hand. "We came to say thanks to you. And to Bathsheba! As you can see — Daniel's fine now!"

"Hi, Lizzy. Hi, Daniel!" James and Mandy replied, delighted to see that the toddler looked none the worse for his experience.

Daniel gave them a sunny smile. "'Lo," he said. But as soon as he spotted Bathsheba, his mouth dropped open in wonder. He pointed a chubby finger at her. "Look! Pussy cat!"

Mandy and James laughed as Daniel went over and sat on the rug beside Bathsheba. He stretched out his hand and began softly petting her head. Bathsheba purred, enjoying the attention.

"Ooh," Daniel murmured. "Nice pussy cat." He stroked her ears gently, then put his arms around Bathsheba and laid his cheek against her tabby coat.

"Oh, no." Lizzy looked worried as Daniel stretched

out on the rug beside the cat. "I don't know if that's a good idea."

She took a step forward, ready to rescue Bathsheba from Daniel's affectionate embrace. But she needn't have worried. Bathsheba, purring loudly, snuggled up close to the toddler and closed her eyes.

"Look at that," Mandy said in amazement. "She really seems to have taken to him."

"The feeling seems to be mutual," Lizzy said with a chuckle. "I think Daniel's in love!"

"It's a shame that Colin's so against having a cat, isn't it?" James said.

"Walton Church just won't be the same without Bathsheba," Mandy said wistfully.

Lizzy looked uncomfortable. "We'd love to adopt Bathsheba," she said. "*Especially* after what she did for us. I'm sure that if it wasn't for Colin's allergy, he might think differently, but . . ." She lapsed into an awkward silence.

Mandy nodded sadly. But something else was troubling her. Something important, concerning Bathsheba. If only she could remember what it was.

"I wondered if you'd both like to come for an early dinner at the house," Lizzy said, changing the subject. "To say thank you, for all you've done."

"We'd love to, wouldn't we, James?" Mandy said.

James nodded. "You bet!"

"That's settled then," Lizzy said. "How about Saturday?"

"Fine," Mandy replied. "I'll just have to check with Mom —" Suddenly she jumped up. "That's it! I remembered!"

James and Lizzy gaped as Mandy waved her hands about with excitement. "Lizzy, I've got something to tell you. If I'm right, it could solve our problem."

Nine

Mandy began her explanation. "The other day, Colin was so excited about Daniel being okay that he didn't notice Bathsheba. He stood right next to her cage for about ten minutes. And he didn't sneeze once!"

"That's right!" James confirmed.

Lizzy looked thoughtful. "You know — this could make all the difference."

"You mean — Colin might consider adopting Bathsheba?" Mandy asked hopefully, her eyes shining.

"I'm not sure," Lizzy replied. "He still might not want to risk having a cat around. I think we need a plan to persuade him to give it a try. I have an idea, but I'll need some help."

"We'll help, won't we, James?" Mandy said promptly. James nodded. "Of course!"

"All right then," Lizzy said, rubbing her palms together. "How about if, on Saturday, you and James bring Bathsheba with you. I'll make sure Colin's busy, so he doesn't see you arrive. We'll put the pet carrier somewhere in the room, but out of sight."

"That's brilliant!" Mandy said. "Then we'll know for sure whether Colin's allergic to her!"

"Exactly!" Lizzy said. "And if everything's okay, we'll bring Bathsheba out. I don't think there'll be any objection to us adopting her after that!"

James was grinning from ear to ear. "I just hope it works!"

"Me, too!" Mandy said with feeling.

"It's settled then." Lizzy went over to Daniel, who was still curled up with Bathsheba. "Time to go now, Daniel. Mommy has to do some shopping on the way home. Say bye-bye to Bathsheba."

Daniel's bottom lip quivered ominously. "Want to stay with pussy cat!"

"I know you do. We'll see her again very soon," Lizzy promised. "But she needs to sleep now. Come on, little man."

Rather reluctantly, Daniel stood up. "Night-night, pussy cat."

"He misses that creamy gray cat that used to visit us," Lizzy observed. "He still looks out for it. But it seems to have stopped coming now. Anyway, see you on Saturday. How about five o'clock?"

"We'll be there," Mandy and James said.

Lizzy and Daniel made their way out. As soon as Mandy had seen them off, she dashed back indoors. "I've got to tell Mom and Dad about our plan!"

Dr. Adam and Dr. Emily chuckled when they heard the details. "That's what I call devious," Dr. Adam said.

"No, Dad," Mandy insisted. "It's called gentle persuasion! I think Bathsheba's as good as adopted!"

"Hmm." Dr. Emily gave her daughter a steady look. "I just hope you and James aren't counting your chickens."

On Saturday morning, Mandy ate a hurried breakfast. As soon as she'd finished, she rushed to the residential unit to do her chores.

She mopped floors, cleaned out cages, and changed water in dishes. It might not be interesting or exciting work, but it had to be done.

"Finished!" she announced an hour or so later as she ran back into the kitchen.

"I take it you have the rest of the day all planned?" her dad guessed as she tugged off her boots and stood them on some newspaper.

"Yup! James is coming over. Then we're going to get Bathsheba ready to go."

"Oh, yes. It's delivery day, isn't it?" Dr. Adam smiled. "I'll drop you over there if you like. What time are you going?"

Mandy told him. "We have to be on time. Lizzy's going to make sure that Colin's occupied when we arrive."

"Yes, ma'am." Dr. Adam clicked his heels and did a mock salute. "Your chauffeur will be standing by!"

Mandy searched for a grooming brush, then went into the living room and curled up on the sofa. Bathsheba jumped straight onto her lap. As Mandy brushed her, the tabby purred contentedly.

"Your coat's looking much better already," Mandy murmured. "And James can't complain — you smell just fine now!"

Bathsheba made a "brup" sound of approval. Mandy chuckled, rubbing the cat behind her ears. Part of her felt sad that she wouldn't be looking after the tabby for much longer. But if Lizzy's plan worked, Bathsheba would be back in her rightful place and she and James would be able to go and visit her.

James arrived, just before lunchtime. He took a package out of his coat pocket. "I picked up my photos on the way over."

"Oh, great," Mandy said. "Let's go and show them to Mom and Dad."

Dr. Emily was making lunch. "It's only tomato soup and sandwiches because I imagine you'll be having a fair amount of food later."

"That sounds great. Thanks, Dr. Emily," James sat down and took his photos out of their envelope. He passed them around.

"These are really good," Dr. Adam said, looking at the different views of the church. "I wouldn't be surprised if you get an 'A' for the art project."

James blushed and played with his glasses. "I hope so. But it wasn't just me. Mandy helped."

"And if you hadn't been taking photos, we would never have noticed Bathsheba running into the church after the stone-colored cat!" Mandy said.

"Oh, yes. Whatever happened to that other cat?" Dr. Emily put bowls of soup on the table.

Mandy shrugged. "I don't know. Lizzy says she hasn't seen it for a while. And I haven't dreamed about it for ages now — not since Bathsheba came back," she said thoughtfully.

Dr. Adam winked at her. "I've a feeling we've seen the last of the mystery cat."

*   *   *

"I'm just going to feed Bathsheba before we leave," Mandy said, a few hours later. "She usually falls asleep the moment she's finished eating."

"That's a good idea," James said. "Then we won't have to worry about her meowing and spoiling our plan."

Once they were ready to go, Mandy lifted the tabby into the carrier. Bathsheba settled down at once and tucked her nose into her paws.

"Okay then. All set?" Dr. Adam came into the room, jingling his car keys.

James nodded, pulling on his coat. "I think I'll take my photos. Lizzy and Colin might like to see them."

There wasn't a sound from Bathsheba during the journey to Walton. Mandy felt nervous and excited at the same time. The Land Rover pulled up in front of the house, and Mandy and James got out.

"Enjoy yourselves — and good luck!" Dr. Adam said. "I hope the plan works. Give me a call if you need a ride back."

"Thanks, Dad," Mandy said. "I've got my fingers and toes crossed!"

The front door opened and Lizzy appeared. "Come on in. Colin's upstairs with Daniel."

She led Mandy and James into the kitchen. She had been cooking, and the whole room smelled wonderful.

Mandy saw that measurements for the new cabinets and shelves had been taken, but the decorating wasn't finished yet. A pile of long wooden planks was stacked against one wall.

"I thought we'd tuck Bathsheba away behind this wood," Lizzy said.

"Okay." Mandy put the pet carrier there.

Lizzy took Mandy's and James's coats. "Make yourselves at home. I'll just go and tell Colin and Daniel you're here."

Daniel came running into the kitchen a few minutes later, followed by Colin, wearing jeans and a bright red sweater.

"Hello there. Nice to see you two again!" he said warmly. "I hope you've got good appetites. Lizzy's cooked enough for an army!"

"Where pussy cat?" Daniel said expectantly, looking around with a big smile on his face.

"Mandy and James have left Bathsheba at Animal Ark," Colin explained to his son.

Daniel frowned and shook his head. "Want see pussy cat!"

Uh-oh. Mandy threw James an anxious glance. She

sensed a tantrum building. If Daniel insisted on searching the room for Bathsheba, he'd give the game away.

Lizzy stepped forward quickly and swept up the toddler. She plunked Daniel in his high chair and gave him a little pile of sliced cheese. "You and cats!" she said affectionately, kissing his cheek. "That's all you think about!"

Distracted, Daniel giggled and began delicately picking at the cheese and eating it strand by strand.

"Phew! That was close," James said, just loud enough for Mandy to hear.

"Is everyone ready to eat?" Lizzy began putting food on the table.

Mandy and James offered to help. *So far, so good*, Mandy thought as she put out plates. *Not a single sneeze from Colin.*

There was macaroni and cheese and grilled tomatoes, followed by cookies and spicy carrot cake. Lizzy certainly could cook.

"That was wonderful. Thanks, Lizzy," Mandy said, half an hour later.

"Yup, it was great," James agreed. "I couldn't eat another thing."

"It must have been good then," Colin joked.

James, shy as usual, reddened. "I've brought my photos with me. Would you like to see them?"

"I'd love to," Colin said. "In a minute, though, if that's okay, James. I've something to tell you all first."

Lizzy looked at her husband in surprise. "What's this, Colin? Have you been keeping secrets?"

"Who, me?" Colin grinned. "Never. But I've come to a decision and I thought I'd wait until today to tell you all. It's about Bathsheba —"

"Oh." Mandy held her breath. *Now what?*

"I want us to adopt her," Colin said. "After what she did for us, she deserves to have a home here. I know what I've said in the past, but I'm prepared to put up with the sneezing and sniffles —"

"But you won't have to —" Mandy burst out, before she could stop herself.

"Uh-oh," James said. "That's it!"

Colin looked at them both. "What do you mean?"

"Oh, this is wonderful!" Lizzy started laughing. "Looks like the cat's out of the bag!"

Mandy and James began to laugh, too.

Colin scratched his head, looking bemused. "Would anyone like to tell me what's going on?"

"Why don't we show him?" Mandy said, jumping up. She got the carrier and brought it over to Colin.

Colin's jaw dropped as Mandy took Bathsheba out and put her on the floor.

"Look!" Daniel gave a shriek of delight and clapped his hands. "Cat! Cat!"

"Just a minute," Colin said. "Has that cat been in the room since you arrived?"

Mandy nodded. "We brought her with us."

"But I'm not sneezing. My eyes aren't running."

Lizzy chuckled. "No. Because you're not allergic to Bathsheba! Mandy said you weren't. But we wanted to be sure. We were going to try to persuade you to adopt Bathsheba, but we didn't need to."

"No!" Mandy said. "You'd already decided to do that — all by yourself!"

Colin looked as if he couldn't believe it. "Hang on." He looked at Mandy, James, and Lizzy's innocent faces. "If I'm not mistaken, there's been some kind of a conspiracy going on here! Okay, you guys. Time to confess!"

Two minutes later Colin knew everything. "Ha, ha, ha!" he belted. "Oh, this is priceless. You guys all ganged up on me."

Lizzy went over and gave him a hug. "You big softie," she said. "You really would have put up with your allergy, wouldn't you, so we could adopt Bathsheba?"

"A man's gotta do what a man's gotta do," Colin said in a Texan drawl.

"That's the worst impression I've ever heard!" Lizzy giggled. "I wouldn't give up the day job, if I were you!"

Mandy felt like jumping for joy. Their brilliant plan had backfired, but everything had worked out for the best. Bathsheba had a home for life!

Daniel was petting the cat's head with an expression of pure delight on his little face. Bathsheba was basking in the attention. Her wheezy purr seemed to fill the room. Lizzy poured some milk in a saucer and put it down for Bathsheba.

"Just for a special treat," she said. "Cats shouldn't have milk very often. It isn't good for them, is it, Mandy?"

Mandy smiled and shook her head. She could see that Lizzy and Colin were going to be caring and responsible owners. And Bathsheba would, once again, be a familiar figure during services in Walton Church.

Colin wiped his eyes. He seemed to have recovered now. "Wow — all this excitement's too much! James, didn't you mention some photos a while ago?"

"Oh, yes. Here they are." James passed them around.

"These are good." Colin said, leafing through them, "especially the ones taken in the crypt." He was studying one of the photos particularly closely. "Wait a minute. Now, that's really strange."

"What is?" Lizzy asked.

She got no answer. Colin rose to his feet. "Come with me, all of you," he said excitedly. "I want you to see this for yourselves."

Colin unlocked the church door and led Mandy, James, Lizzy, and Daniel down the steps to the crypt.

Mandy shivered. After the cozy kitchen, the crypt was cold and gloomy. Colin didn't seem to notice. Flashlight in hand, he hurried straight over to the largest tomb, which was covered with a carving of the first reverend of Walton.

"Look at this," Colin said. "Have a good, close look. Tell me what you see."

Mandy and James looked at the stone carving.

"It's the first reverend of Walton," James began uncertainly. "He's lying there with his hands together as if he's praying."

"He's wearing a hooded robe," Mandy added. "And there's a sleeping cat curled up by his feet —" She stopped. There seemed to be something strangely familiar about that stone cat.

"Exactly! The cat!" Colin cried. "That's it. Now — take a look at this!"

Lizzy came over to see for herself as Colin held up James's photo. The stern-faced reverend was depicted in splendid detail — the folds in his robe, the beauti-

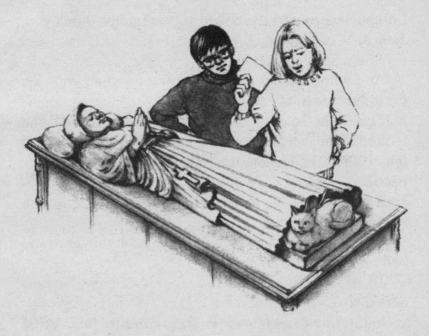

fully carved hands — but there was no cat lying near his feet.

Mandy did a double take. She ran her eyes over the photo again. No. She wasn't mistaken. "Oh," she said. "But that's impossible. James — look. There's no cat in your photograph!"

James frowned. He looked at the tomb, then back at his photo. "I don't get it. What's going on?"

"You took your photos of the crypt the day before

Bathsheba came back and led you to Daniel, didn't you, James?" Colin asked.

Mandy and James nodded.

"And who was Bathsheba running to when you saw her returning to the church?"

"The stone-colored cat." Mandy replied. Then she looked at the sleeping cat on top of the stone tomb and felt a shiver of realization. "The *stone* cat!" she whispered.

Everyone looked at the statue, then back at the photo.

"The stone cat brought Bathsheba back to where she belonged!" Mandy continued.

"To where she was needed. To save Daniel," James added, awestruck.

Colin shook his head. "It seems impossible. But I can't see any other explanation."

Lizzy looked as if she couldn't take it all in. "It's incredible," she said. "It really is. But would anyone mind if we continued this conversation in the kitchen? Daniel's getting a bit cold down here."

"You go in, hon," Colin said. "We'll follow you in a minute."

"You know," James said, walking around the tomb to look at the first reverend of Walton's harsh face. "I don't think this guy was so bad after all."

"Why's that?" Mandy asked.

"Well, he was a cat lover, wasn't he?"

Mandy and Colin laughed.

"That makes him okay in your book, does it?" Colin said with a twinkle in his eye.

"Oh, yes," Mandy said with feeling. "All the best people love animals!"

"Seems like I'm off the hook, too, then!" Colin laughed. "Come on. Let's go back into the house. I think we all need a hot drink to warm us up."

Colin made his way back toward the crypt steps. James followed him.

Mandy took one last look over her shoulder. "Thank you for bringing Bathsheba back and saving Daniel," she said softly to the sleeping stone cat. "I'll probably never know where she was — or how you did it — but thank you anyway."

Somehow, Mandy knew for certain that no one would be seeing the mysterious stone-colored cat around Walton churchyard again. Its task was done, and it could once again rest between the feet of its beloved master.

As Mandy left the crypt, she glanced up to where Bathsheba's cat gargoyle was looking down. James and Colin came and stood beside her.

In the fading light, it almost looked as if the cat were smiling.

TM

Look for the next spooky
Animal Ark ^{TM} *Hauntings title:*

DOG IN THE DUNGEON

"Do you think we should?" James asked, glancing up at the window. It was pitch-black and the castle was eerily quiet, except for the persistent howl of the unknown animal.

"Come on, James," Tilly pleaded, blowing out the candle and snapping on the electric light. "This is a great adventure. We won't come to any harm."

Mandy stood up and pulled on her shoes. "Well, I'm more *worried* about that poor creature out there than frightened. It sounds as though it might need help to me. Come on, James. If we go together with Blackie, we'll be fine — we've got to find out what it is!"

"I was hoping," mumbled James, getting up reluctantly, "that we wouldn't hear it tonight." He looked across at Blackie, pacing back and forth below the window, looking unusually nervous. He began to pant slightly. Mandy hadn't seen Blackie do this before. He was always up for anything and more than eager for a challenge.

"It's not that I don't want to investigate, it's just that Blackie seems so . . . uncertain . . . as though he knows something, somehow, that we don't," James explained.

Ignoring James's protestations, Tilly grabbed a powerful flashlight from the depths of a grubby-looking knapsack. She put a finger to her lips and opened her bedroom door, which creaked alarmingly. Mandy, James, and Blackie followed her out. Their rubber-soled sneakers were soundless on the wooden floors as Tilly led the way to the top of the staircase. Blackie slunk along beside them, walking as though he expected the floor under him to cave in at any moment. He seemed very nervous.

"Why not take him back to the room?" Tilly said in a hushed voice. "He's going to wake the whole place with those tip-tapping claws of his."

James reluctantly did as Tilly suggested, shutting the door behind Blackie, saying, "You'll be better off in there, boy."

Mandy walked silently behind Tilly, glancing at the distorted shadows dancing on the walls in the light of her swinging flashlight. They found a light burning in the hall at the base of the stairs. Tilly plunged on excitedly, into the dark passage and beyond. Twice she paused, listening for the sound of howling, following it for clues to its source.

"It's coming from below us!" James whispered.

"There is a door to the side of the kitchen, and I know a flight of stairs leads to what my grandfather *thinks* is a cellar," Tilly said. "We'll try there."

Mandy couldn't tell if she was terrified or excited, but her heart pounded steadily as James and Tilly tried to budge the heavy wooden door. The moment it opened the sound of the animal howl could be heard loudly and clearly. "Howooooo . . ." It came floating up the stairs and echoing off the walls, as though someone had suddenly turned up the volume on a radio.

"Somebody," whispered James, "is playing a trick on us. This is a joke. There simply *can't* be an animal stuck down here!"

But James was whispering to Tilly's back. She was already leaping down the stairs in great excitement. Mandy noted how fearless her new friend was and, ignoring her own rising nervousness, followed quickly after her, with James on her heels.

At the bottom, the beam of Tilly's big flashlight showed a small, unused room without furnishings, except for a large, carved wooden chest. It smelled dusty and musty and made Mandy cough. Tilly swiveled the beam slowly around the bare stone walls. The howling had stopped.

"Are we dreaming, or what?" Tilly said softly.

There, in a corner, an enormous dog was sitting calmly and expectantly on the floor. It had the same smallish head and elegant body of a greyhound, only a bit larger, and with a thick, ragged pale blue-gray coat. It sat still, gazing at Mandy, James, and Tilly with a sort of quiet dignity. It seemed to be sizing them up.

"A deerhound!" Mandy breathed.

"How on earth did it get down here?" Tilly said, amazed.

"Who can it belong to?" James whispered.

"It looks just like the dogs in the paintings!" Mandy said. "It's one of the Aminta dogs!"

"Well, it isn't going to attack us, that's for sure. It looks as gentle as a lamb. I wonder how long it's been trapped down here?"

"It couldn't have been long. It doesn't look thin or anything," James observed. "Perhaps it belongs to someone who keeps it in here and comes to feed it."

"That's cruel!" Mandy said. She moved past Tilly and

cautiously took a step toward the dog. But nothing about the great dog's expression or behavior seemed threatening. It didn't get up, or growl, or bare its teeth.

"Hello, you sweet thing," Mandy spoke gently, and held out her hand. The dog stood up, and took a step backward. Mandy saw that it had a snow-white mark in the shape of a diamond on its chest. "We're not going to hurt you," she told it softly. "Come on and say hello. Good dog."

"Definitely mysterious," James said. "I mean, it's not frightened or angry, it isn't wounded or sick — so what's it doing sitting down in this chilly old room making all that noise?"

The dog took a few steps toward the wooden chest. It moved gracefully, almost as though it were gliding. Again, Mandy reached out, shuffling slowly forward on her haunches, a low hand outstretched. "Here, boy." But again the dog moved back a pace out of Mandy's reach, still looking steadily at her.

"I can't see a water bowl or any food around, can you?" Tilly asked, flicking her flashlight around the corners of the room. The dog now began to sniff, then paw at the wall against which the big chest was standing. It looked up at Mandy and tilted its head, then pawed at the wall again, making a scraping on the stone with its claws that made Mandy's hair stand on end.

Tilly crouched low and aimed the beam of her flashlight on the dog. "It's a girl dog," she announced. "Anyone can see that."

"She doesn't want us to touch her, but I think she's asking us to open this chest!" Mandy guessed.

James came forward. "Shine your light on the bolt, Tilly." He bent down and examined it. "Hmm, it's padlocked — no hope of opening it." The dog had backed off into the shadows when James had approached. Now she came slowly forward, put out her elegant front paw and scraped at the wall again.

"No, she wants us to move it!" cried Tilly. "Let's push it over — she's lost a ball or something, I bet, behind it."

James pushed hard against the chest with his forearms. It gave easily, sliding along on the smooth stone floor. "Look!" breathed Tilly. "There in the wall!" A small, bolted opening about one square yard had been revealed.

James tugged at the bolt, working it back and forth until it opened with such force that it knocked him back onto the floor. Laughing, Mandy and Tilly helped him up. "Wow," he said. He turned around to look up at Tilly. "Maybe we should get your grandfather, or someone."

"No, not yet," Tilly said. "I vote we go in and take a look."

DOG IN THE DUNGEON

"Shine your light over there first, Tilly," said James. "Let's see where the dog is. Oh, look, she's gone. She's gone through the door."

"She couldn't have, James," Tilly said. "The door isn't even completely open yet." The unbolted door had swung open only a few inches. She shone the light around the room, directing its beam into all the corners. The dog had gone.

"This is *weird*," said James, with a shudder.

Tilly was on her hands and knees, the metal casing of her flashlight hitting the stone. She had pulled open the doorway and was starting to crawl through it. Her voice came back to them from the other side of the wall, sounding as though she was speaking with tissue paper in her mouth. "She's here waiting for us. Come through. Oh! It's a dungeon!"

Mandy and James had been plunged into sudden and complete darkness.